CLUB TIMES

For Members' Eyes Only

Bachelor Beware!

There must be something in the water to cause all these pregnancies and marriages in Mission Creek. I've done some initial testing in my love laboratory, but results are inconclusive. Oh, I'm pulling your leg, members. I'm no scientist, but I have put three of the LSCC's cleaning ladies on "Wedding Ring Watch" to smoke out the bachelors. By the way, Clay Martin, we're giving you a head start! Some lucky gal's gonna lasso you sooner or later!

Isn't Daisy Parker doing a swell job serving you all? Why, it seems only months ago we had a time of it understanding her Texas twang, and now she's like family. Last thing, Daisy, we'd like to recommend Rosie's hair salon near the edge of town. They do a great dye job on some of the local ladies, so you don't have to worry so much about your roots.

I won't name names, but the rascally daughter of Ford Carson was found in someone's back seat the other night. An LSCC gardener was watering the rosebushes when he heard some giggling in the north parking lot. He's been sworn to secrecy about the identity of the lady in question, but c'mon, we all know who it was....

As always, members, make your best stop of the day right here at the Lone Star Country Club!

D0980953

About the Author

PEGGY MORELAND

published her first romance with Silhouette in 1989 and continues to delight readers with stories set in her home state of Texas. Peggy is the winner of a National Readers' Choice Award, a nominee for the *Romantic Times* Reviewer's Choice Award and a two-time finalist for the prestigious RITA® Award. Her books frequently appear on the *USA TODAY* and Waldenbooks bestseller lists.

Though Peggy has written over thirty books for Silhouette, *An Arranged Marriage* is her first experience in coordinating her efforts with such a large number of talented authors. She found the process both intriguing and challenging, and enjoyed researching the duties of the Texas Rangers organization.

When not writing, Peggy can usually be found out on her ranch, tending the cattle, goats and other critters she and her husband raise. You may write to Peggy at P.O. Box 1099, Florence, TX 76527-1099, or e-mail her at peggy@peggymoreland.com.

PEGGY MORELAND

AN ARRANGED MARRIAGE

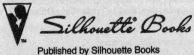

Silhouette Books

Published by Silhouette Books
America's Publisher of Contemporary Romance

Special thanks and acknowledgment are given to Peggy Moreland for her contribution to the LONE STAR COUNTRY CLUB series.

SILHOUETTE BOOKS

ISBN 0-373-61358-X

AN ARRANGED MARRIAGE

Visit Silhouette at www.eHarlequin.com

Printed in U.S.A.

Welcome to the

LONE STAR
LSCC
COUNTRY
CLUB
EST. 1923

Where Texas society reigns supreme—
and appearances are everything.

They came from very different worlds...
but had more in common than they ever imagined.

Clay Martin: He's the only man in Mission Creek who can rein in a bratty little princess. So when the great Carson patriarch makes him an offer he can't refuse...an offer involving money, marriage and a beautiful future wife...Clay is definitely up for the challenge.

Fiona Carson: She's spent her entire life getting what she wants, especially from her daddy. And although men have always fallen at her feet, her "husband" is not so easily swayed. Could it be that the spoiled heiress has met her match—and fallen head over heels in love?

Tyler Murdoch: A mercenary on a dangerous mission, he's been sent into the jungles of Central America and must rely solely on his skills and courage to keep him safe. But will he also be able to protect the gorgeous Hispanic interpreter who's been sent to assist him, and who has become a *major* distraction?

THE FAMILIES

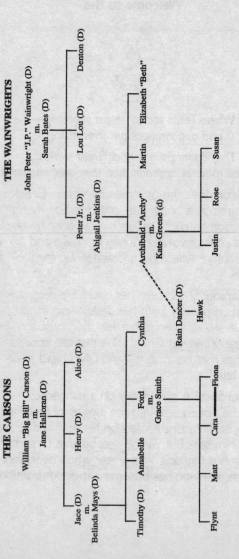

THE CARSONS

William "Big Bill" Carson (D)
m.
Jane Halloran (D)

- Jace (D)
  m.
  Belinda Mays (D)
- Henry (D)
- Alice (D)

- Timothy (D)
- Annabelle
- Ford
  m.
  Grace Smith
- Cynthia

- Flynt
- Matt
- Cara — Fiona

THE WAINWRIGHTS

John Peter "J.P." Wainwright (D)
m.
Sarah Bates (D)

- Peter Jr. (D)
  m.
  Abigail Jenkins (D)
- Lou Lou (D)
- Denton (D)

- Archibald "Archy"
  m.
  Kate Greene (d)
- Martin
- Elizabeth "Beth"

Rain Dancer (D)
- Hawk

- Justin
- Rose
- Susan

D   Deceased
d   Divorced
m.   Married
----- Affair
| Twins

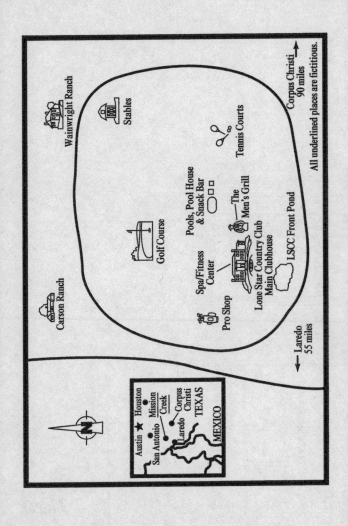

Wainwright Ranch

Carson Ranch

Stables

Golf Course

Pools, Pool House
& Snack Bar

Spa/Fitness
Center

The
Men's Grill

Tennis Courts

Pro Shop

Lone Star Country Club
Main Clubhouse

LSCC Front Pond

← Laredo
55 miles

Corpus Christi
90 miles ↑

All underlined places are fictitious.

Austin ★

Houston •

Mission
Creek •

San Antonio •

• Corpus
Christi

• Laredo

TEXAS

MEXICO

N

One

Mission Creek, Texas, was no booming metropolis by any stretch of the imagination. Tucked between Corpus Christi and Laredo, its origins dated back more than a hundred years, when it was nothing more than a trading post for the ranches surrounding it. In spite of its modest size and humble beginnings, the town was filled with enough crime, corruption and scandal to keep the scriptwriters for *Law & Order* in new material for years. Perhaps even enough to justify the filming of a *Godfather IV,* since the mob was involved in the majority of the shady goings-on around town.

Most of the dramas played out at the Lone Star Country Club, a two-thousand acre spread situated on land donated by the Carsons and the Wainwrights, two of the area's earliest families to settle here. Oddly enough, the donation of the land might well have been the families' last friendly venture, since the Carsons and the Wainwrights had been locked in a feud that stretched as far back as most folks' memories.

The recent marriage of Matt Carson and Rose Wainwright hadn't ended the feud or lessened the hatred, but it had served as a momentary distraction from a six-month-old mystery—or scandal depending on the results of paternity tests a certain golfing foursome was undergoing. Or at least three of them were. The fourth, Luke Callaghan, absent from that particular morning's round of golf, was currently in a military hospital in Central America, recovering from injuries he'd received while trying to rescue his former military commander from terrorists, and was unaware that he'd been targeted for a paternity test.

A baby left on the ninth tee of the golf course for the father to find was shocking news even for a Peyton Place like Mission Creek. The note attached to the infant, with the only decipherable words being "this is your baby girl," had everyone in town laying bets as to which one of the golfing foursome had sired the abandoned child and clucking their tongues over the unidentified mother's lack of maternal instincts.

Murder? Corruption? An abandoned baby?

This wasn't the Mission Creek Clay Martin remembered from his youth, and it certainly wasn't the peaceful environment he'd sought when, disillusioned with life, he'd ended his military career early, accepted a job as a Texas Ranger and made the long trek back to Texas. But changed or not, Mission Creek was home, and Clay was determined to do his part in bringing law and order back to the town.

At the moment, though, he was officially off duty and nursing a beer at the bar in the Lone Star Country Club's Men's Grill. The building itself was a temporary structure built to replace the original Men's Grill destroyed by a bomb several months prior. In spite of its stopgap status, the bar still managed to reflect the discriminating tastes of the club's wealthy members.

Unfortunately Clay wasn't one of them.

By all rights, he knew he could be arrested for trespassing. Only card-carrying, dues-paying members were allowed admittance to the prestigious country club's facilities, and Clay didn't have the pedigree or the portfolio to even apply—two small details he didn't see changing any time in the foreseeable future.

The rich get richer, while the poor keep digging themselves deeper and deeper into debt, he thought with more than a little resentment. That was one thing about Mission Creek that hadn't changed over the years.

The sharp *clack* of pool balls being hit carried from an adjoining room, followed by a loud whoop, grabbing Clay's attention. The Billiard Room, he thought with a huff of disgust as his gaze settled on the stained-glass sign hanging above the arched opening. Why the hell couldn't they call it what it was, instead of slapping a fancy, five-dollar name on it? It was a pool hall, the same as hundreds of other smoke-filled rooms he'd frequented around the world, where men hung out, drinking beer and shooting eight-ball with their buddies.

But those other pool halls hadn't been outfitted with leather chairs, heavy brass light fixtures and etched glass, he reminded himself as he gave the room a cursory glance.

With a woeful shake of his head, he drained his

beer, then lifted a finger, signaling the bartender to bring him another. Within seconds a pilsner of foaming beer was sitting in front of him. Clay chuckled as the bartender moved away.

Member or not, it seemed when a Texas Ranger asked for something, he got it. Fast.

With the exception of the money this particular Texas Ranger needed to hold on to his family's ranch.

His amusement faded at the reminder of his current financial woes. Curling his fingers around the glass, he scowled at the golden liquid, wondering how in hell he was going to come up with the money he needed to turn his family's ranch into a profitable business. Not on a Ranger's salary, that was for sure.

If he'd been smart, he told himself, he'd have socked away more of the money he'd earned while serving in the Special Forces branch of the army. But, no, he'd foolishly squandered his pay trying to impress Celine Simone, a wealthy heiress, whom he'd even more foolishly made the mistake of falling in love with.

"Women," he muttered under his breath. "Nothin' but trouble."

"I'll drink to that."

Clay glanced over to find Ford Carson sliding onto the stool next to his, his glass lifted in a silent toast of agreement. Clay tapped his glass against Ford's. "You got women trouble, Mr. Carson?"

Frowning, Ford plucked the skewered olive from his

drink and tossed it aside. "Daughter trouble, to be exact."

Clay didn't have to ask which of Carson's twin daughters was causing him problems. Fiona's escapades were known all over town. "And what has Fiona done this time?"

Ford's face, already florid, flushed an unhealthier red. "The damn girl went out and bought herself a brand-spanking-new Mercedes. Didn't even ask my permission. Just sashayed over to the dealership, signed a check on my account and drove the blamed car right off the lot!" Dragging a hand through his thick shock of white hair, he shook his head wearily. "I tell you that girl is going to be the death of me. I don't know what the hell to do with her anymore."

Ordinarily Clay would have let the comment pass without comment, but the thought of anyone frittering away tens of thousands of dollars when he was so desperately in need of money infuriated the hell out of him. "If she were my daughter, I'd cut off her access to my bank accounts, then march her butt right back down to that dealership and make her return the car."

Ford angled his head to peer at Clay. "You would?"

Clay gave his chin a decisive jerk. "Damn straight. What she did was totally irresponsible and disrespectful of the privileges you've obviously allowed her."

"And you think that would teach her a lesson?"

Clay lifted a shoulder. "Maybe. Maybe not. Fiona's

what? Twenty-seven?'' At Ford's nod, he shook his head. "Pardon me for saying so, Mr. Carson, but Fiona's had things her way for so long it may take more than a slap on the hand to bring her around."

Ford's frown deepened. "You're probably right. A headstrong young woman like Fiona won't break easily."

The two stared at their drinks, both silent as they contemplated their individual problems. After a moment Ford glanced Clay's way. "I haven't seen your sister, Joanna, around town lately. She hasn't moved, has she?"

Smiling, Clay shook his head. "No, sir. She's in Europe for the summer, touring with a group of her French students."

"Glad to hear it. I'd hate for Mission Creek to lose such a fine teacher."

"No worse than I'd hate losing my sister," Clay replied. "She's only been gone a week and I already miss her."

Ford nodded slowly, then glanced Clay's way again. "Didn't I hear you bought back your family's ranch?"

"Yeah," Clay replied. "Though keeping it might present a problem."

"How so?"

Embarrassed to admit to his strapped financial condition, especially to a man as wealthy and successful as Ford Carson, Clay kept his gaze on his beer. "Unless I can figure out a way to raise the cash to make the improvements needed to turn the place into a profitable business again, I stand to lose it.''

"I wouldn't toss in my cards just yet," Carson said.

Feeling the intensity of the man's gaze, Clay glanced up to find Ford studying his reflection in the mirror behind the bar.

"What if I were to give you the money you needed to get started?" Ford suggested.

"*Give* me the money?" Clay repeated.

"Well, not *give*," Ford amended. "A little trade."

Clay snorted. "And what would you want of mine in trade? My truck? The shirt off my back? That's about all I've got left, after buying back the home place."

Ford flattened his lips in disapproval. "Don't sell yourself short, son. You've got a lot to offer in trade. You're responsible, hardworking, honest. And you're tough and brave, to boot. You proved that during your stint in the army, and again when you chose to move back to Mission Creek. Not many men would've had the guts to return to the town that was ready to hang him."

Clay stiffened at the reminder of the charges filed against him for the murder of his girlfriend when he was twenty-three. "I have nothing to be ashamed of. I didn't kill Valerie. That was proved in court before I ever left town."

"Just the same," Ford maintained, "it took guts to come back here."

Not liking the direction the conversation was taking,

Clay asked impatiently, "What does all this have to do with you giving me money, anyway?"

"A trade," Ford reminded him, then softened the reminder by clapping a hand on Clay's shoulder and giving it a squeeze. "You have traits I admire, son. Traits I'm willing to pay for."

Clay shook his head, wondering if the beer was clouding his thinking, or if Ford Carson truly wasn't making a lick of sense. "Sorry, but I'm afraid I'm not following you."

"I want you to marry my daughter," Carson said, then held up a hand when Clay choked a laugh. "This is no joke, son," he warned. "I'm willing to pay you a hundred thousand dollars if you'll agree to marry Fiona and teach her the meaning of responsibility and commitment. Two months," he said, before Clay could interrupt. "You have to remain married for two months—although it would probably be best if we kept that time restriction from Fiona. I'll give you half the money once you're legally married. The other half when the two months are up. At that time, if you choose, you'll be free to file for a divorce and resume your bachelor life."

Clay stared at Carson, unable to believe the man was serious. A hundred thousand dollars? he thought, trying to absorb the magnitude of the offer. A hundred thousand dollars would go a long way toward rebuilding his family's ranch. And all he had to do to get the money was agree to marry Fiona Carson and stay married to her for two months?

It was insane, he told himself. Ludicrous. Fathers didn't arrange marriages for their daughters anymore. Especially not when the daughter was Fiona Carson. She'd never agree to this, he told himself. Fiona was wild as a march hare and stubborn as a mule.

She was also Clay's only viable hope of holding on to his family's ranch.

"And Fiona will go along with this?" he asked doubtfully.

"She won't have a choice," Ford replied confidently, then chuckled. "Of course, she won't know the real purpose of the marriage. She's stubborn. Takes after her old man in that way. If she knew that I'd arranged for you to marry her to teach her responsibility, she'd dig in her heels so deep it would take a team of Clydesdales to drag her to the altar."

"If not the truth, then what do you intend to tell her?"

Ford puckered his lips and thought for a moment, then shook his head. "Beats the hell out of me. But I'll think of something."

When Clay's expression remained skeptical, Ford shot him a wink. "Don't worry about Fiona, son. She'll play along. I'll see to that."

Though probably a fool for not accepting the offer on the spot, Clay continued to hesitate. He'd always believed that a man made his own way in the world, never seeking the easy way out of a tight situation. And marrying a woman for money was definitely the coward's way out of his current cash problem.

Frowning, he shook his head. "I don't know, Mr. Carson. I need to give this some thought."

Carson rose and tossed a business card onto the bar. It landed face up beside Clay's hand. "Take all the time you need," he said. "That's my private number. Give me a call when you've made your decision."

Dusk was settling over the countryside by the time Clay arrived home later that evening. Instead of going inside as he'd intended, he detoured to the gate that led to the back pasture. Bracing his arms along its top, he stared out across the land. Not so long ago, a herd of registered Brangus cattle would have been grazing there on fertile coastal grass. Now the pasture was empty but for the knee-high weeds that swayed gently in the soft evening breeze, and a scattering of young cedar and mesquite trees.

It hadn't taken nature long to reclaim the land, he thought sadly. Eight years to be exact. He remembered well the backbreaking work it had taken to clear the pastures. Chopping down the cedars and mesquite trees that were such a nuisance to ranchers in this region of Texas. Shredding native brush high and thick enough to conceal a grown deer. Hauling away truckloads of rock to clear the land for the equipment he and his father had used to prepare the soil for planting.

But most of all he remembered all the bitching and moaning he'd done because he'd been forced to help with the work.

With a regretful shake of his head, he opened the

gate and started across the field, his hands shoved deep
in his pockets. As he walked, weeds slapped at his
legs, leaving the sticky seed pods of beggar's lice
clinging to his starched jeans. In the distance a line of
fencing marked the back boundary of his family's
ranch. Choked with vines, the fence was held upright
by an occasional mesquite or cedar tree that had woven its way up through the tangled strands of barbed
wire.

On his left stood the hay barn. Once it had housed
the heavy bales of coastal hay his family had cut and
baled to feed the cattle through the winter. Now the
building stood empty, its wide doors open and sagging, its red-painted walls faded and, in some places,
showing visible signs of rot. Loose panels of tin on
the barn's high roof flapped in the breeze, creating a
mournful sound in the otherwise peaceful evening air.

Clay stopped in the middle of the pasture and turned
slowly, silently acknowledging each sign of neglect
and disrepair. As he did, he wondered what his parents
would say if they could see the ranch now. Emotion
clotted his throat as he realized the answer. If they
weren't already dead, he knew it would kill them.

His parents had loved this place, had put their hearts
and souls into building their home and clearing the
land for the cattle operation that would support their
family. They'd done it for themselves, he knew, but
they'd done it for him and his sister, as well. They'd
wanted to leave their children a legacy, a dream to
carry on.

And Clay had let them down.

At the time of the automobile accident that had taken their lives, he'd just been promoted into the Special Forces unit of the army. He was full of himself and his own importance, and eager to leave his mark on the world. Though he'd returned home for his parents' funerals, he'd left afterward as soon as possible, leaving the handling of the estate in his sister Joanna's capable hands. She'd wasted no time in selling the ranch. Not that Clay had blamed her. Joanna had never cared for the ranch; nor had Clay, for that matter. His love for the place and his appreciation for all that it stood for had come later. Almost too late.

It shamed him now to remember his youth. Growing up, he'd given the term "bad boy" whole new meaning. But no matter how much trouble he'd gotten himself into, no matter how many times he'd thrown his parents' love back in their faces, they'd never given up on him. Even when he'd been accused of his girlfriend's murder, they'd been there for him, standing firm in their belief of his innocence, their faith in him as an honorable man.

It was the memory of their unconditional love that had gotten him through the dangerous and hellish missions the army had assigned him. And it was the power of that love that had given him the strength and will he'd needed to survive mental and physical tortures unimaginable to most men. At his darkest moments, when he was sure the pain he was suffering at the hands of his captors would drive him insane, he'd focus his mind on home, on family and gird himself with the strength and peace that came from the level of unconditional love his parents had given him.

That was what had saved him.

And now he wanted to save the ranch.

Not just for himself, he thought, but for his parents. It was the only way he knew to honor their memory, to prove their faith in him, to carry on their dream. Throughout his darkest hours, the ranch had served as his light, a beacon in an otherwise bleak world, his reason for living. If he lost it now, he feared with it he would lose his last hold on all that was good and merciful.

But how could he hang on to it, he asked himself, feeling the frustration returning, when he could barely afford the monthly mortgage payments, much less take on the tremendous burden of upkeep on a place this size? The bottom line was, the ranch had to pay for itself or he'd lose it. Which brought him right back to his original question: how could he raise the cash he needed to make the ranch a profitable business again?

He dragged off his Stetson and raked his fingers through his hair. He knew the answer. Ford Carson had handed it to him on a silver platter not more than an hour ago. All he had to do was marry Carson's daughter and the money he needed was his.

He slapped his hat against his thigh in frustration. But, dammit, he didn't want to get married—especially not to a spoiled, rich girl like Fiona Carson. He'd been engaged to a woman who had enjoyed a privileged upbringing similar to Fiona's, and he'd learned the hard way that that kind of woman didn't stick and, more, that he didn't belong in that world.

Clay didn't believe in fate or luck. He'd been taught that a man created his own. But how else could he explain Ford Carson's offering him a windfall right when he needed it most? All he had to do to collect the money was marry the man's daughter.

Firming his lips, he slapped his hat back on his head and pulled his cell phone from the clip on his belt. "It's a job," he told himself as he punched in Carson's private number. "Nothing but a job."

At the sound of Carson's voice, Clay narrowed his gaze on the dilapidated barn in the distance, imagining it as it had looked eight years before, and as he hoped it would look again.

"You've got yourself a deal."

"Fiona, I need to talk to you."

Her fingers already curled around the front door-knob of their family home, Fiona glanced over her shoulder to find her father standing in the doorway to his study. "Can't it wait, Daddy? I'm supposed to meet Roger at the Empire Room at eight for dinner."

"No, it can't."

She hesitated a moment longer, tempted to ignore the authoritarian tone in her father's voice. She was an adult, after all, wasn't she? She didn't have to jump every time he snapped his fingers.

When she continued to hesitate, he lifted a brow—

a slight movement, but one Fiona had learned meant business. With a huff, she dropped her hand from the knob and marched across the entry. "If this is about the car again..." she began irritably.

He stepped aside, allowing her to enter the study before him. "No. It's not about the car." He seated himself behind his desk and gestured toward the leather sofa opposite him. "Have a seat."

She twisted her wrist and gave her diamond-studded watch a pointed look. "I'd rather not. I don't want to keep Roger waiting."

"Why not?" he asked dryly. "It's never seemed to bother you before to keep a man waiting."

Before she could respond, he held up a hand. "What I have to say won't take long." Frowning, he leaned back in his chair and studied her from beneath dark brows. "I'm worried about you, Fiona."

She rolled her eyes, sure that she was in store for another lecture on her many shortcomings. "Daddy—"

"And about me," he said, cutting her off. "My health, specifically."

That silenced Fiona as nothing else could. She looked closely at her father, noting for the first time the floridity of his skin. "Is it your heart?" she asked, terrified that he might be suffering complications from the heart surgery he'd had several years before. "You've been taking your medicine, haven't you?"

"Yes, I've been taking my medicine," he snapped. "But I'm not getting any younger, Fiona, and neither are you. Unfortunately you aren't showing the signs of maturity normally associated with a woman your age. You're twenty-seven years old, unemployed and seem content to let me support you for the rest of your life."

Fiona rolled her eyes again. "I've told you before, there isn't any job that interests me." She turned for the door. "We can talk about this later. I've got—"

"Hold it right there, young lady!"

When she turned, a brow arched in surprise at his angry tone, he pointed at the sofa. "We're talking about this *now*."

She hesitated, again tempted to defy him, then pursed her lips and flopped down on the sofa. "Okay," she said, slapping her arms across her chest. "I'm sitting. So talk."

He sank back in his chair, suddenly looking older than he should, defeated. "I'm worried what will become of you if something were to happen to me."

She dropped her arms, tears springing to her eyes. "Oh, Daddy," she said, scooting to the edge of the sofa. "Please don't talk that way. Nothing's going to happen to you."

"But something *could*," he insisted gruffly. "And frankly it concerns me that you are so ill prepared to take care of yourself."

She stiffened in indignation. "I can take care of myself!"

"How?" he challenged. "Where would you live? How would you support yourself? You've never worked a day in your life. I doubt you have even a clue how high maintenance you are.''

She sniffed, offended. ''I had no idea you considered me such a burden. I thought you enjoyed having me around.''

''I do enjoy having my children nearby,'' he said in growing frustration. ''And believe me, I miss Cara now that she's gone. But I've made it too easy for y'all.'' He leveled a finger at her nose. ''Especially you. I've allowed you to remain dependent on me, when you should have been out on your own years ago. But I'm rectifying that mistake.''

''Rectifying?'' she repeated, fearing that her father had found her a job. ''How?''

''I've arranged for you to be married.''

She shot to her feet. ''Married!'' she cried.

''Yes. Married. It's the only way I can be assured you'll be taken care of in the event of my death.''

She laughed weakly. ''You're kidding, right? You're just trying to bully me into getting a job and moving out.''

He shook his head. ''This is no joke, Fiona. I'm serious about this. *Dead* serious.''

She sank to the sofa, her knees suddenly too weak to support her. ''Daddy, no,'' she whispered. ''You can't do this to me.'' She leaped to her feet as the ramifications of his announcement fully hit her. ''You can't force me to get married! I won't do it.''

''You will. I've already made all the arrangements.''

Her chin jerked up. "And who, exactly, have you chosen for me to marry?"

"Clay Martin."

"Clay Martin!" she echoed in dismay. "But he's so…so…"

He lifted a brow. "Poor?" he offered.

She clamped her lips together, refusing to admit that was the very word she'd been searching for. "He's a murderer," she said, instead. "Do you hate me so much that you would marry me off to a murderer just to get me out of your house?"

"Clay isn't a murderer. You know as well as I do that he wasn't responsible for that girl's death."

Fiona turned away, wringing her hands, trying to think of a way out of this mess. When she couldn't, she whirled and thrust out her chin again. "I won't marry him, and there's nothing you can do to make me."

He lifted a brow and leaned forward to push a folder across the desk. "I wouldn't be so sure."

Fiona stared at the cream-colored folder, her stomach doing a slow, nauseating flip as she recognized it as the one in which her father kept her financial records. "What do you mean?"

"I'm canceling all your credit cards and closing your bank account. Plus, I'm notifying the bank that, in the future, you're not to be allowed to write any more checks on my account. You, my dear daughter," he said, looking a little too pleased with himself, "are broke. Penniless. *Poor.*"

She curled her hands into fists. "You wouldn't dare."

"Oh, yes, I would. I'll continue to give you a monthly allowance, but it will be deposited into Clay's account, not yours. He will have full control of the funds and will be instructed to dispense them to you as he sees fit."

The idea of asking any man for spending money, especially Clay Martin, made Fiona positively ill. She searched her mind for an escape hole. "What about Clay?" she asked, grasping at the first thought that came to her. "Surely he hasn't agreed to this ridiculous plan of yours."

Ford stood, his smile smug. "Oh, but he has. In fact," he added, his smile broadening, "he seems as anxious as I am for this marriage to take place."

Two

Judging by Fiona's behavior that night at the Empire Room, no one would have guessed that her life was about to drastically change. Dressed in a form-fitting, black silk tank top and matching capris that revealed an enticing amount of cleavage and leg, she laughed and flirted with every man who stopped by the table she shared with her date, Roger Billings.

And after dinner, when she and Roger left the dining room to finish their bottle of wine by the adult pool, not a male in the place would have suspected that Fiona's days as Mission Creek's most sought-after female were about to end. Understandable, since their minds were dulled by the sensual sway of her hips as they followed her departure with their gazes.

Not so understandable was the fact that her date was unaware of her state of panic.

Stretched out on a lounge chair by the pool, Fiona glanced Roger's way. No surprise there, she thought resentfully. Roger Billings was the most narcissistic man she'd ever had the misfortune to meet.

If she hadn't already decided to dump him, his attentiveness that evening—or lack thereof—would have convinced her to end their two-week-old relationship. She never would have pursued him in the first place if she hadn't overheard that snotty old Angela Forsyth bragging in the spa that she'd have him at the altar within a month of his divorce settlement, claiming that he was the catch of the year.

Catch of the year, my eye, she thought peevishly. The man was so tight he squeaked, and he was an unmitigated bore. When he wasn't complaining about his ex-wife taking him to the cleaners in their divorce settlement or about the outlandish fees the court-ordered therapist was charging to counsel his three children, he was talking about himself, crowing about all his accomplishments.

She glanced his way again as he paused in his monotonous monologue long enough to drain the wine from his glass. When he reached for the bottle—the cheapest vintage listed on the wine menu, no less—to refill it, it was all she could do to keep from snatching the bottle from his hand and bopping him over the head with it.

Didn't he realize she needed some help here? A distraction? Something, anything, to keep her mind off the bomb her father had dropped on her earlier that evening!

An arranged marriage, she thought furiously. How utterly archaic! And to Clay Martin, no less. Had her father lost his mind?

And why had he singled out *her* to inflict his cruelties on? Threatening to close her bank and credit-card accounts. Of all the nerve! There had to be something she could do to prevent him from doing this to her. But what? Though she'd thought of little else since he'd informed her of the ridiculous arrangement, she hadn't been able to come up with a single workable plan.

Which was amazing, really, now that she thought about it. Ever since she was in diapers, she'd been able to find a way to get around her father. On those rare occasions when she couldn't, she'd simply thrown a tantrum until he'd finally given in.

But she was too old to get away with holding her breath until she turned blue, she thought miserably. At any rate, she feared a tantrum wouldn't work for her this time. When he'd delivered his ultimatum, she'd detected a distinct and unwavering resolve in her father's voice that she'd never heard there before, one that had chilled her to the bone.

He wouldn't back down this time, she told herself dejectedly. Her carefree days were about to end.

She lifted a brow. Or were they? There was a third party involved in this ridiculous scheme. Clay Martin. There was still a chance that *he* might change his mind—especially if she was to give him a little something to make him question his agreement to marry her. Something really risqué. Something downright scandalous.

And before her lay the perfect setting to create just such a scandal.

She sat up and turned to look at Roger, her face flushed with excitement. "Let's go skinny-dipping."

He choked on his wine. "Wh-what?"

"Skinny-dipping!" She swung her legs over the side of the chair and stood, reaching behind her to unfasten the waist of her capri pants, her enthusiasm for her plan building as she imagined Clay's reaction when he heard of her latest escapade. And he'd hear about it all right. She'd make sure of that.

Roger stared, his eyes widening, as she wiggled her pants to her ankles and stepped out of them. Swallowing hard, he looked up at her. "B-but what if someone sees us?"

Pulling the tank top up and over her head, she shook out her long hair. Since she hadn't bothered with a bra, she was left wearing nothing but a black lace thong. Curving her lips in a sultry smile, she braced her hands on the arms of Roger's chair and leaned to press her mouth to his.

She withdrew slowly to meet his gaze, slicking her tongue over her moist lips. "That just adds to the thrill, doesn't it?" she said huskily, then laughed and ran for the pool. At the edge, she executed a near-perfect dive into the crystal clear water and surfaced mid-pool, still laughing as she scraped her hair back from her face. Her laughter faded when she saw that Roger stood at the side of the pool fully dressed.

She treaded water. "Aren't you coming in?" she asked in surprise.

He glanced uneasily around. "I don't know, Fiona. If someone were to see us..."

"So what if they do?" she returned boldly. "We're

adults.'' She rolled to her back and stroked farther away, sure that he would join her. When he didn't, she treaded water again. Frustrated that he wasn't co-operating, but confident that she could persuade him to join her, she purred. ''Umm. The water feels absolutely decadent on my hot skin.''

She peeked through her lashes to check Roger's re-action and saw that his face was flushed and his eyes were riveted on her breasts. Convinced that he was weakening, she pushed her arms out in a modified breast stroke and swam toward him. When she reached the side, she folded her arms over the tiled edge and looked up at him, tipping her head to the side. ''Don't you want to go swimming with me?'' she asked, puck-ering her mouth in a Shirley Temple pout she knew from experience men found hard to refuse.

He swallowed hard, his gaze fixed on the mounds of flesh squeezed between her folded arms.

''Come on, Roger,'' she coaxed as she pushed away from the side. ''No one will see us. I promise.''

She watched his Adam's apple bob again, then shrieked when he jumped in fully clothed, splashing her with a tidal wave of water. He surfaced several feet away.

''See?'' she said, laughing. ''Doesn't the water feel marvelous?''

He didn't reply. Instead, he started swimming to-ward her. It was then that Fiona noticed the feral gleam in his eyes. She pushed her arms against the water, backing away from him, wondering if perhaps she might have been a little impulsive. "Roger…" she warned as he neared.

He grabbed her, catching her by her upper arms.

"Roger!" she cried, struggling to twist free, as he pulled her to him. "What are you doing? Let me go!"

Instead of releasing her, he locked his arms around her, making escape impossible.

"If you don't let go of me right this instant," she said furiously, "I'll—"

"You'll what?" he challenged.

Before she could answer, he dropped his mouth down on hers, smothering any hope of a reply. Truly frightened now, she flattened her hands against his shoulders and shoved, but was unable to break his grip. She felt the ironlike jab of his arousal against her abdomen and fear iced her veins.

Remembering a defense technique her brother Matt had taught her, she lifted a knee and rammed it as hard as she could between his legs. He bent double, groaning and holding himself.

"How dare you!" she accused furiously, then spun in the water and swam for the side. She'd almost made it out of the pool, when he caught her arm and tugged her back.

She clawed at his hand, trying to pry his fingers loose. "Roger!" she cried. "Let me go!"

He swung around to brace his back against the side of the pool, pulling her with him, then locked his arms around her again. "Come on, Fiona. Just give me a little kiss."

"Roger, please," she begged, straining away from him. "Let me go."

"You heard the lady. Let her go."

Startled, Fiona glanced up and saw a man standing on the side of the pool directly above them, his legs spread wide, his hands braced on his hips. Although his face was shadowed by a silver Stetson, she knew her rescuer immediately. The khaki slacks with the knife-sharp creases. The starched white shirt with the silver Texas Ranger badge pinned to the front pocket. Dark brown cowboy boots with a shine so high she could see her reflection in them.

Clay Martin, she thought, relieved that she was being rescued. Then she realized her luck. She couldn't have planned this better if she'd plotted for weeks!

"Get lost," Roger growled, then jerked Fiona close again.

Instead of fighting him this time, she wrapped her arms around his neck, prepared to put on a show.

"What the—"

Fiona stumbled back as Roger's arms were torn from her and watched wide-eyed as Clay hauled him from the pool by the back of his collar. She stared, stunned by the bulge of muscles straining beneath the sleeves of Clay's shirt as he dragged Roger onto the tiled apron of the pool.

Cursing, Roger fought to sit up. "What the hell do you think you're doing? We were just having a little fun."

Clay planted a boot in the middle of Roger's chest

and pushed him back down. Folding his arms across
his thigh, he leaned to peer down at him.

"Now, nobody enjoys a good time more than me,"
Clay informed Roger in that slow Texas drawl of his.
"But when there are two parties involved, and especially when one of them is a lady, both parties have
to be having a good time before it can be considered
as such. You may disagree with me, but it didn't appear to me that Fiona was having much fun."

Scowling, Roger shot a hand beneath his nose. "It
was her idea," he grumbled. "*She's* the one who
wanted to go skinny-dipping, not me." He flung his
hand in Fiona's direction. "Ask her yourself if you
don't believe me."

Clay angled his head to look at Fiona. The eyes that
met hers were black as night and hard as stone. It was
all she could do to keep from shrinking away.

"I don't doubt that for a minute," Clay said. He
turned back to smile at Roger. "Fiona does seem to
have a fondness for making a public spectacle of herself."

She sucked in an indignant breath. "Now wait just
a minute!"

Clay went right on talking as if she hadn't spoken,
as if she wasn't even present. "But I do question her
willing participation in what followed."

"Well, what did she expect to happen?" Roger demanded. "Standing there buck naked and begging me
to get into the pool with her. You tell me what you

would've done, Ranger, if you were caught in a similar situation.''

Clay pulled at his chin thoughtfully. "Now, that's hard to say, since a woman's never objected to me kissing her."

Roger huffed out a breath. "The mighty Texas Ranger," he muttered. "The whole damn lot of you are nothing but a bunch of gun-toting, self-righteous, macho cowboys." He gave Clay's boot an angry shove. "Would you get your damn foot off my chest? You're restricting my air supply."

"I'll be happy to oblige—just as soon as you give me your word that you won't repeat what transpired here tonight."

"And why the hell would I want to make a promise like that?"

"Because a lady's reputation is at stake," Clay replied. He turned his head and gave Fiona a long look, one that sent a shiver chasing down her spine, then added, "And that lady happens to be my future wife."

Clay stood with his hands braced on his hips, watching to make sure Roger didn't have a change of heart before he made it to the parking lot.

"Well?" came Fiona's indignant voice from behind him. "Are you going to stand there all night or are you going to hand me a towel?"

Clay glanced over his shoulder to find her still standing chin-deep in water. Though her hair floated in wet, tangled clumps around her shoulders and mascara was smeared beneath her eyes, she still managed to look beautiful, regal. Untouchable. But then she always had been. Especially for men like Clay Martin.

"Depends," he replied, and turned to fully face her.

"On what?" she snapped impatiently.

"On how nicely you ask me for that towel."

She jerked up her chin. "I'll turn into a prune first."

He lifted a shoulder. "Suit yourself."

She glared at him a full five seconds, then narrowed her eyes in challenge and began pushing her way through the water toward the steps. Clay watched as first her bare shoulders appeared above the surface, then her chest. Water sluiced down her pampered flesh, leaving droplets to cling to the tips of her nipples, making them glitter like diamonds in the moonlight. Shaking his head, he dragged a towel from the back of a chair and moved to the edge of the pool. As she climbed the steps, he spread his arms, holding the towel open for her.

She stepped onto the tiles, then turned and waited, her chin tipped high, as if she were a queen, the towel her royal robe and Clay a lowly servant there to do her bidding. With a slowness meant to infuriate her, he draped the towel around her shoulders and brought the ends together, tucking them between her breasts.

He heard her sharp intake of breath as his forearms grazed her nipples, felt the swell of her breasts beneath the thick terry cloth. Unable to resist, he cupped his hands over her shoulders and dipped his mouth close to her ear. "Cold?"

Though he could feel the tension in her, the awareness, her expression revealed neither as she turned slowly in his arms.

"No," she said in a voice set on a seduction. "Actually, I'm rather hot." She stepped closer and pressed a fingertip against the center of his chest. Tipping her head to the side, she looked up at him through lashes still spiked with water and smiled. "Want to cool me off, Ranger?"

Her voice was breathy, seductive, but Clay knew her too well to fall for the coquettish act. "I suppose I could throw you back in the pool," he offered.

He caught the flash of temper in her eyes before she masked it. Pretending indifference, she flicked a nail beneath his chin and turned from his arms. "Your loss, Ranger."

Clay watched her walk away, unable to help noticing the provocative sway of her hips beneath the damp towel. Feeling a pang of sympathy for Roger, he shook his head and followed. "What were you trying to prove, Fiona?"

She turned and let the towel drop. "When?" she asked innocently.

Though it was difficult, Clay managed to keep his eyes on hers and not follow the towel's descent. "Earlier with Roger. You can push a man only so far, you know, before he's gonna expect you to deliver the goods."

She struck a seductive pose. "So what's your breaking point, Ranger?"

Clay slid his gaze slowly down her body, noting the puckered nipples, the tiny V of damp black lace that clung to her femininity. He shifted his gaze back to hers. "I don't know. Want to test me and see?"

She pursed her lips and studied him a moment as if considering, then fluttered a hand and turned away. "I would, but I'd really hate to ruin your macho image."

He snorted a laugh. "Yeah, right." Stooping, he picked up the towel and held it out to her. "Who was the show for, Fiona? Me or your father?"

She snatched the towel from his hand. "Who said I was putting on a show?"

Clay pinched his khaki slacks just above the knees and sank down onto the foot of the lounge chair. "Call it an educated guess, but when a woman strips down to her unmentionables and persuades a man to go skinny-dipping with her, then kicks up a fuss when he tries to score…" He lifted his hands. "Well, that would make a person question the woman's motives."

She whipped the towel around her and flopped down on the chair beside him, angrily tucking the ends between her breasts. "You think you're pretty smart, don't you."

He bit back a smile as he leaned forward, bracing his elbows on his knees, and looked out over the pool. "Doesn't take a genius to figure that one out." He spared her a glance. "So who were you trying to piss off? Me or your father?"

She dropped her gaze to her lap, frowning as she plucked at a loose loop of thread on the towel. "You," she admitted reluctantly. "Daddy's a lost cause. Once he's made his mind up about something, there's no changing it."

Clay nodded slowly, knowing she wasn't exaggerating. Fiona was famous for her stubbornness, but as her father had said, she'd come by it honestly. She'd inherited it from him. "Sure appears that way."

She continued to pluck at the loose thread, then angled her head to look at him suspiciously. "The one thing I can't figure out is how he talked you into going along with this insane scheme of his."

Clay looked away, narrowing his gaze on the water, reluctant to admit that it was greed that had motivated him. But if nothing else, Fiona deserved honesty from him, at least on this one aspect of his and Carson's agreement.

"Money."

Her eyes widened in surprise. "Daddy *paid* you to marry me?"

He nodded.

"How much?"

"A hundred thousand."

She shot to her feet. "A hundred thousand dollars!" she exclaimed.

At his nod, she whirled and stalked away. She stopped at the edge of the pool and slapped her arms across her chest, smoke all but coming out her ears.

"You should have held out for more," she called over her shoulder. "I bet he'd have paid much more than a piddling hundred thousand to get rid of me."

Hearing the hurt in her voice, the bitterness, Clay remained silent, unsure how to respond.

She spun to face him. "So when are we supposed to tie the knot?"

Clay lifted a shoulder. "He didn't name a date."

"Then let's do it tonight."

"Tonight?" he repeated in surprise.

"Yes, tonight. If I know Daddy, he'll want a big church wedding. It'll serve him right if we spoil his fun."

A big church wedding? Clay hadn't considered that possibility when he'd accepted Carson's offer. The idea of a church full of people witnessing him promise to love, honor and cherish Fiona until death do them part was an image too brutal to consider.

"We'd have to go across the border into Mexico," he said, mentally thinking through the details required for a rushed marriage. "It would take days to get the blood tests and license required by the state."

"Mexico doesn't require those things?"

"Depends on who you know."

Fiona strode back to the lounge chair and ripped off the towel. "Fine," she said tersely, and snatched up her pants. "The sooner we get this over with, the better, as far as I'm concerned."

Clay shifted in the leather bucket seat, trying to find a more comfortable position for his backside. It was impossible. Compared to his truck's roomy bench seat, the bucket seats in Fiona's car seemed the size of peanut shells.

He should have insisted on taking his truck, he told himself. But one look at his mud-splattered pickup and Fiona had refused to put a foot inside and had demanded that they take her car to Mexico, instead.

The Mercedes, he thought bitterly, flexing his fingers on the luxury automobile's leather-wrapped steering wheel. How ironic. Here he was driving the very car whose purchase had put Ford Carson over the edge, provoking him into arranging a marriage for his daughter and sentencing Clay to a two-month stint as her warden.

He glanced across the console at Fiona. She still assumed the same angry posture she had throughout their trip, with her face turned to the passenger window, her arms folded across her chest and her left shoulder hunched high against him, warding off any attempt he might have made at conversation.

Fine, he told himself, as he turned his gaze back to the road ahead. Let her sulk. His job was to teach her responsibility, not to entertain her. Keeping one hand on the wheel, he pulled his cell phone from the clip on his belt and quickly punched in Benito's number again.

"We've cleared the border," he told his contact, whom he'd called earlier that night to make the necessary arrangements for the marriage. "What's your twenty?" He listened, scanning the dark road ahead, then said, "Yeah. I see you. Lead the way." He pressed the disconnect button, then clipped the phone back at his waist.

A truck swerved onto the highway from a side road ahead, its headlights slicing through the darkness as it fishtailed onto the lane in front of them. Clay slowed, giving Benito the lead. He followed the rattletrap truck through the quiet streets, down a narrow alley and braked to a stop behind it. He climbed out of the car, giving Benito and the man who accompanied him a nod of greeting as the two approached the car.

"Hey, *amigo*," Benito said, grinning and giving Clay a slap on the back. "Long time no see."

Clay nodded. "Yeah. It's been a while. Is everything ready?"

"*Sí,*" Benito assured him. He gestured toward a heavy door, set into the adobe wall. "The magistrate, he is waiting inside." Clay glanced at the shadowed entrance, then braced a hand on top of the car and leaned to peer inside. "Okay, Fiona. This is it."

Without sparing him a glance, she pushed open her door.

Somewhere along the way, she'd primped a little, removing the telltale signs of her skinny-dipping adventure. Probably when she'd gone into the service station where he'd stopped for gas, Clay decided. Her hair was dry now and wound on top of her head, a silver comb holding it in place. She'd also removed the mascara streaks from beneath her eyes and had slicked her lips with some glossy kiss-me color.

But if she'd made the effort for Clay, she'd wasted

her time. It would take a hell of a lot more than a hairstyle and makeup to impress him.

But Benito didn't seem to need anything more. He watched her climb from the car, his mouth gaping. *"Mi Dios,"* he murmured, unable to tear his gaze away. "This one, she is beautiful." He glanced at Clay. "How did you ever talk a beautiful *señorita* like this into marrying an old *hombre* like you?"

Scowling, Clay started for the front of the car to meet her. "It was her father's idea."

He took Fiona by the elbow, intending to escort her inside, but she jerked free of his grasp. After giving him a scathing look, she strode toward the heavy wooden door, her nose in the air.

Chuckling, Benito moved to stand beside Clay, as he watched Fiona storm away. "She is a wild one, *sí, señor?"*

With a grunt, Clay followed her. "You haven't seen anything yet."

The room they entered was small, the only illumination provided by two fat columns of wax set in iron sconces on the far wall. A long wooden table stood beneath the flickering candles, a silver crucifix jutting from its center. To the right of the crucifix lay a couple of sheets of paper—the official marriage documents, Clay assumed. On the wall to Clay's left, a colorful drape of fabric covered an arched doorway.

As he noted the covering, the drape was pushed aside and a short, dark-skinned man entered the room. Benito quickly made the introductions. Clay shook the magistrate's hand, but Fiona kept her arms stubbornly folded across her chest and her gaze fixed on the wall, refusing to acknowledge the introduction.

With a weary sigh, Clay said, "Let's get this over with."

The magistrate gave him a curious look, but moved to stand before the table and gestured for the others in the room to gather around him. Once again Clay took Fiona by the elbow to guide her into place. This time, surprisingly, she didn't pull away.

The magistrate slipped a small leather-bound book from the folds of his serape and began the ceremony. Clay focused his gaze on the crucifix, trying not to think about the promises he made, as at the magistrate's prompting, he offered the appropriate "I do's."

"Usted puede besar a su esposa."

Clay snapped his gaze to the magistrate, then stole a glance at Fiona, wondering if she understood enough Spanish to realize that the magistrate had just given Clay permission to kiss his bride. He didn't have to wonder long. She seared Clay with a look that would have stopped a herd of stampeding cattle in their tracks, then pushed past the magistrate and snatched the papers from the table.

"Where do I sign?"

After indicating the place for her signature, the magistrate quickly moved out of her way. She scrawled her name, tossed down the pen, then marched from the room, slamming the door behind her.

Benito crossed himself, then looked at Clay, his brown eyes soft with sympathy. "May God be with you, my friend."

Three

Fiona slept curled in the passenger seat, her head resting against the tinted window, her hands folded beneath her cheek. In sleep, she looked almost innocent. Angelic.

But Clay knew better. Fiona Carson was a spoiled little rich girl, who'd made a career out of breaking men's hearts.

And now she was his wife.

Scowling, he turned his gaze back to the road. The ink wasn't even dry on their marriage certificate, and he was already questioning his sanity in getting involved in this deal. If the past four hours were any indication of what he had to look forward to, he was going to earn every penny Carson had agreed to pay him.

Two months, he reminded himself, and he could divorce her and get on with his life. Two months weren't all that long. He'd spent longer periods of time living in conditions unfit for a pig, endured tortures that would have killed a lesser man and lived to tell it.

And he'd survive marriage to a spoiled rich girl, too. He had to if he wanted to save his ranch.

A set of headlights appeared in the oncoming lane. Clay dimmed the Mercedes's high beams, glancing to the left as the car passed by. Noting that the vehicle was a patrol car, he shifted his gaze to the rearview mirror just as the cop made a tire-squealing three-sixty and raced up behind him, red lights flashing. Frowning, Clay slowed and pulled onto the shoulder.

Fiona stirred on the seat beside him.

"Are we home?" she asked sleepily.

Clay lowered his window. "Not yet."

Stretching catlike, she sat up with a groan. "Then why did you stop?"

His gaze on the rearview mirror, Clay jerked his head, indicating the car behind them. "Highway patrol."

She glanced over her shoulder as the patrolman approached the driver's-side window, flashlight in hand.

Clay recognized the patrolman as Todd Carey, a new recruit on the force and a Texas Ranger wannabe. The kid had the desire to make a good Ranger some day, but he lacked experience, a requirement he was actively pursuing while working for the highway patrol.

"What's the problem, Todd?" Clay asked.

Todd directed the flashlight on Clay's face, making Clay squint.

"Ranger Martin?" he said in surprise. "Is that you?"

Frowning, Clay shoved the blinding flashlight away from his face. "Yeah, it's me. Is there a problem?"

Todd snatched off his hat and jerked to attention, revealing sandy-red hair shaved regulation short on the sides and a face full of freckles. He looked like Opie of Mayberry. "No, sir. At least, none that I'm aware of." He peered around Clay to look at Fiona. "Just checking on Miss Carson."

Fiona graced him with a smile that would've melted butter off a block of ice. "Hi, Todd. How are you?"

He blushed and shuffled his feet, obviously smitten. "Fine, Miss Carson. Just fine."

"Still working the night shift, I see."

"Yes, ma'am. Though I'm supposed to start pulling days next month."

"Oh, no," she moaned. "That means they'll put Harley back on night duty, and he isn't nearly as nice as you."

Todd swelled his chest and gave his pants a cocky hitch. "Don't you worry none about Harley. If he gives you a hard time, you just let me know. I'll take care of him."

She graced him with yet another dazzling smile and batted her eyelashes at him. "Thanks, Todd. You're the best."

Clay followed the exchange, amazed at Fiona's ability to turn on the charm. Much more, and she'd have Todd drooling.

Todd took a step back from the car. "I guess I better let you folks be on your way." He dipped his knees to look at Fiona. "You might want to give your daddy a call," he warned. "He sounded pretty worried."

"Will do. Thanks, Todd."

Clay pushed the button to raise the window. "Call your daddy?" he repeated.

She brushed at a speck of lint on her slacks, avoiding his gaze. "Yes. He's such a worrier. If I'm not home by the time he thinks I should be, he calls the police." She huffed out a breath. "You'd think I was sixteen and late for a curfew, rather than twenty-seven and more than capable of taking care of myself."

Clay shook his head as he unclipped his cell phone and offered it to her. "What a waste of the taxpayers' money."

She folded her arms across her chest, refusing to take the phone. "I couldn't agree more."

He looked at her in confusion. "Aren't you going to call him?"

She turned her face to the passenger window, jutting her chin stubbornly. "Let him worry. Serves him right."

With a shrug, Clay hooked the phone back to his belt, then put the car into gear and pulled back onto the highway. "Whatever you say."

Fiona pressed her nose to the passenger window, only now becoming aware of her surroundings.

"This isn't the way to my house," she said.

Clay turned into the lane that led to his family's ranch house. "No, but it is to mine." He stopped in front, the headlights spotlighting the modest one-story ranch-style house, built of native limestone.

She stared, then slowly turned to look at him. "You expect me to live *here?*"

Though his pride took a hit at the disgust in her tone, Clay could almost understand her shock. Fiona had lived her entire pampered life in the Carsons' palatial mansion, where the household staff outnumbered the family members by more than four to one. Hell, his house would fit in one wing of the Carson home with room to spare.

But this was his home, dammit, he thought defensively, and if it didn't match up to her highfalutin standards, that was just too damn bad.

"Unless you're planning on establishing separate residences, you are." He switched off the ignition and climbed from the car. Without waiting to see if she followed, he headed for the back door.

Once inside, he flipped on the overhead light in the kitchen and tossed the car keys onto the breakfast table. As he did, he heard the familiar squeak of wood on the porch steps and knew that Fiona wasn't far behind.

The slam of the door confirmed it.

"And what am I supposed to do for clothes and toiletries?" she demanded angrily.

He headed down the hall. "You didn't mind swimming in the nude, so I'm sure you won't mind sleeping that way, either."

She sucked in a furious breath, then stalked after him, her hands fisted at her sides. "And a toothbrush? What am I supposed to do about that?"

He stopped at a narrow door, opened it and began pulling out linens. "Use your finger."

"My finger?"

He brushed past her and started down the hall again. "Yeah. Your finger. That's what folks use when they have to make do."

Shaking with rage, she marched after him. "It wouldn't have hurt you to stop by my house long enough for me to pack a bag."

He shoved open a door and hit a light switch with his elbow before stepping inside. "It's late and I'm tired."

"Well, so am I!"

He tossed the linens and pillow onto a bare mattress. "Then you shouldn't have any trouble sleeping." He pointed to a door. "The bathroom's through there. Towels are in the cabinet behind the door."

He turned to leave, but she grabbed his elbow, stopping him. He set his jaw and slowly turned. "What now?"

"Where are you going?"

He jerked his elbow from her grasp. "To my room. Your daddy paid me to marry you, not to sleep with you. Any more questions?"

She folded her arms across her chest. "Just one. Who's going to make my bed?"

"Sorry," he said, brushing past her, "but it's the maid's night off. Guess you'll have to make it yourself."

Putting all her muscle into the effort, Fiona strained to pull the last corner of the fitted sheet over the edge of the mattress. She was within inches of succeeding when the band of elastic snapped from her hand. The loss of tension sent her stumbling backward, and she sat down hard on the floor.

Tears stung her eyes. *I don't know how to make a bed!* she wailed silently. Anita, her family's housekeeper, had always taken care of the household chores at the Carson estate, supervising the staff in the weekly changing of linens and the daily making up of the beds. Fiona wasn't expected to do anything but stay out of their way, which she was more than happy to do.

She sniffed back the tears. But Anita wasn't here, she reminded herself miserably, and if the bed was going to be made, she'd have to do it. Clay certainly wasn't going to help her.

The tears burned hotter at the thought of Clay. She hadn't given the details of their marriage much thought, hadn't had the time, but it had come as a shock to discover that he intended for them to maintain separate bedrooms. Not that she wanted to sleep with him, she assured herself. In fact, she'd looked forward to setting him straight on that aspect of their marriage the moment he made the first move toward intimacy.

Unfortunately he'd robbed her of that opportunity…and wounded her feminine pride in the process.

She narrowed her eyes at the unmade bed, then

snatched the sheet and pillow from the floor and pushed to her feet. Well, he'd learn soon enough that Fiona Carson didn't accept that kind of treatment from any man, husband or not. She might be married, but that didn't mean she had to *act* like a wife. In fact, she didn't see any reason why her lifestyle should change at all. Her address and her last name might have changed, but *she* wasn't changing.

Calmer now and feeling a bit more in control, she crawled onto the bare mattress, pulled the sheet up to her chin and snuggled her cheek against the pillow.

A hand closed over Fiona's shoulder and gave her a hard shake.

"Time to get up."

Startled awake, she flipped open her eyes at the unexpected male voice, then groaned, melting back against her pillow, when she recognized the voice as Clay's and remembered where she was. Rolling onto her back, she pushed her hair off her face to squint up at him. "What time is it?"

"Seven."

She rolled to her stomach with a groan and dragged the sheet over her head.

He gave her a slap on the behind. "Come on, Fiona. Up and at 'em. I've got to get to work."

"So go," she wailed pitifully.

"In case you've forgotten, we left my truck at the country club. Unless you want to be without wheels for the day, you're going to have to take me to pick it up.''

Stuck out in the sticks by herself all day? She dragged herself from the bed. ''Fifteen minutes,'' she told him, as she stumbled her way to the bathroom.

''Make it five. I've got things to do.''

Fiona took twenty just to spite him.

Clay pulled up alongside his truck and parked. Reaching into his pocket, he pulled out his key ring. ''I should be home about six,'' he told her as he separated one key from the others. ''Here's the key to the house. Make yourself a copy while you're in town.''

Fiona turned to look at him, but her gaze snagged on the sign in front of the car that pointed toward Body Perfect, the country club's day spa. A day at the spa, she thought with a pleasurable shiver. God, that sounded marvelous. Already imagining herself stretched out on a massage table in one of the soothing, pastel-painted rooms, while Victor worked the weariness from her aching muscles with his clever hands, she turned up her palm.

''I'll need money.''

''For what?''

''A massage.''

He lifted a hip and reached for his wallet. ''How much?''

''Five hundred ought to do.''

His eyes rounded. ''Five hundred *dollars?*''

She gave him a withering look. ''No, pennies.''

Scowling, he pushed his wallet back into his pocket. "Not on my watch," he muttered, and pushed open the door.

Fiona leaned across the console. "Your watch? What is that supposed to mean?"

"Nothing. Just an expression."

"Hey!" she called when he turned away. "What am I supposed to use for cash?"

He pulled out his wallet again, plucked out a bill and tossed it onto the driver's seat. "Make it last," he warned before slamming the door.

Fiona snatched up the twenty-dollar bill and slumped back into her seat, glaring at him through the windshield as he climbed into his truck and drove away. "Twenty dollars," she muttered under her breath. That wouldn't even cover her tips.

She slapped down the sun visor, then winced as she was confronted with her reflection in the vanity mirror. Drawing a tube of lipstick from her purse, she smoothed some over her lips, then angled her head and fluffed her hair, evaluating the admittedly weak attempt to improve her rumpled appearance. With a sigh of resignation, she dropped the tube back into her purse, pushed open her door and stepped out into the early-morning sunshine.

Shoving her sunglasses over the bridge of her nose, she strode across the parking lot and along the fragrant garden path to the frosted glass entrance of Body Perfect.

Ginger Walton, the attendant that morning, glanced

up from the reception desk as Fiona breezed into the room. Though normally a waitress at the country club, Ginger looked comfortable filling in for the spa receptionist, who'd taken a leave.

"Well, good morning, Fiona," she said in surprise. "You're out awfully early this morning."

Fiona blew a breath up at her bangs and pulled off her sunglasses. "Tell me about it."

"Do you have an appointment?"

"No, but I was hoping you might be able to squeeze me in."

Ginger picked up a pen and frowned over the appointment book. "We're pretty well booked for the day, but I'll see what I can do. What do you want to have done?"

Fiona pressed her hands against her lower back and the aching muscles a night sleeping on the lumpy, bare mattress had left her with. "The works, starting with a massage."

"Lucky for you, Victor's nine o'clock canceled. You can have your massage first, then I'm sure Lucille or one of the other girls can work you in for a manicure, if you'd like."

"Marvelous!" Fiona headed for the dressing room to don one of the spa's lush terry robes, but stopped, her hand on the door. "Oh, and Ginger," she called over her shoulder. "Would you be a dear and order a grilled-chicken caesar salad and a glass of that yummy peach-flavored iced tea delivered here at noon?" She laughed gaily, her mood improved dramatically now that she knew she'd be spending the day at the spa. "And check and see if you can arrange for me to have one of those seaweed and herbal wraps. After the night I've spent, my body is just screaming for rejuvenation."

Clay didn't carry a Day-Timer or own a Palm Pilot. In his line of business, he found it safer—and a hell of a lot easier—to keep all his information in his head. Thankfully he'd been blessed with a razor-sharp memory and an uncanny knack for recalling series of numbers that made carrying around an address book and daily calendar unnecessary. Before going to bed each night, he'd simply think through the cases he was working on, make a mental list of the tasks he needed to accomplish and the people he needed to contact the next day, then close his eyes and enjoy a restful night's sleep, confident that when he awoke, he had only to call the list to mind, and he was ready to hit the ground running.

His current caseload was heavy, as were those of most of the Texas Rangers, filled with everything from unsolved murder cases in his region of Texas to those dealing with international crimes. He did keep a set of files on both current and past cases, though he considered the required paperwork a royal pain in the ass. Those files he kept at home, in the bedroom he'd commandeered as his office, the one he'd slept in as a boy.

Though he was part of a specialized, statewide organization of law-enforcement officers, he usually worked alone. Personally he preferred it that way. As the old saying went about the Texas Rangers, "One riot, one man."

After dropping off Fiona and picking up his truck, he wove his way through the club's parking lot and pulled his to-do list to the front of his mind. His first order of the day was to track down Flynt Carson and pass on some information—information that had nothing to do with Clay's job as a Texas Ranger and everything to do with helping Flynt save a man's life.

Though Clay had no direct ties to Phillip Westin, the man Flynt and his buddies—Spence Harrison, Tyler Murdoch, Luke Callaghan and Ricky Mercado—hoped to rescue from a Central American prison where he was being held by terrorists, Clay understood the men's loyalty to their former commander from the Gulf War. It was Westin who had devised the daring plan that had resulted in the five men's escape after they were captured by the enemy and held captive underground for six weeks. Because of his own covert experience and time spent in captivity, Clay understood the kind of bond these men shared and their commitment to rescue their former commander.

But one detail about the exchange had altered overnight—a detail that made Clay hesitant to track down Flynt Carson and relay the information.

Clay had married Flynt's kid sister.

Unsure if Flynt was aware of the deal Clay had struck with Ford Carson and concerned what Flynt would think of Clay marrying his sister, Clay pulled to a stop at the exit from the parking lot to reconsider his order of business for the day. The first thing he ought to do, he told himself, was call Ford and tell him the deed was done.

But he didn't want to be the one to alert Ford to his and Fiona's elopement, unsure of the man's reaction. The rushed marriage was Fiona's idea, not his, so she should be the one to take the heat, if her father was less than excited about the news.

A truck whizzed by on the drive before him, headed for the club. Recognizing the vehicle as Flynt's, Clay decided this was as good an excuse as any to put off calling Fiona's father for a while. He flipped on his directional signal, turned into the drive and followed Flynt to the club's entrance. He pulled to a stop behind him just as Flynt jumped down from the truck's cab.

He rolled down his window. "Hey, Flynt!" he called. "Got a minute?"

Flynt turned, a brow arched in question, then lifted a hand in greeting when he recognized Clay and headed his way. "Morning, Clay," he said.

"Mornin'. How's the baby doing?"

Flynt snorted. "Which one?"

Clay laughed, having forgotten that Flynt's new wife, Josie, was pregnant. "Both, though I was asking specifically about the one you have temporary custody of."

"Lena's doing fine. Spoiled rotten," he added, "but healthy as a horse and happy as a pup with a new bone. I tell you, it's going to be hard as hell for Josie and me to turn the kid over to her father once his identity is established.''

Aware of the DNA testing Flynt and his golfing buddies were undergoing to discover which of the four was the baby's father, Clay said, "Yeah, I imagine it will be. It's a shame your DNA didn't match. Then you could just keep her.''

"Amen to that," he agreed. "We've ruled out Spence, Tyler and Michael O'Day, although we all figured there wasn't much chance Michael's would match, since he isn't a regular in our golfing foursome. That just leaves Luke to be tested.''

"Speaking of Luke," Clay said, his expression growing serious, "I might have something for you.''

Flynt stepped closer to Clay's truck. "What?''

"That little problem you have in Central America?'' he said, clueing Flynt in to the topic and the necessity for secrecy.

Flynt glanced around to make sure no one was within earshot. "Yeah. What about it?''

"I have someone who might be able to help.''

"In what way?''

"I spent a couple of months in Central America myself several years ago and made a few friends. I know one of 'em ought to be able to fix Tyler up with a guide, someone who can show him the lay of the land, if you get my drift.''

In spite of the fact that Clay had kept his comments purposely vague, Flynt's eyes sparked with interest, indicating his understanding. "He'd appreciate that," he said, then added in a low voice, "We all would."

Clay opened his glove compartment and pulled out a pad. "Here's the number of the embassy," he said, jotting it down. He tore off the sheet of paper and passed it to Flynt. "Tell 'em Cowboy sent you. That's the name they know me by," he explained at Flynt's questioning look.

Nodding, Flynt folded the paper and slipped it into his shirt pocket. "I appreciate the help, Clay."

Clay shifted into Reverse, preparing to leave. "No problem."

Flynt's cell phone rang and he held up a finger, indicating for Clay to wait while he took the call.

"Flynt Carson," he said into the receiver. He listened a moment, his eyebrows gathering into a frown.

"No, Dad," he said into the receiver. "I haven't seen her." He listened again, then said, "I'm at the club right now, talking to Clay Martin, but my business here shouldn't take long. Just have to sign off on a few new-member applications, then I can head back to the ranch and help you chase her down."

Uh-oh, Clay thought. Busted.

Flynt listened again, then looked at Clay and shook his head, chuckling. "Dad, I really don't think it's necessary to involve the Texas Rangers. Fiona will show up. She always does."

His smile faded to one of puzzlement and he held the phone out to Clay. "He wants to talk to you."

His gut knotted in dread, Clay took the phone. "Good morning, Mr. Carson," he said into the receiver.

"Is my daughter with you?"

Clay winced at the anger in Ford's tone and cut an uneasy glance toward Flynt. "She was. I just dropped her off at the club."

"Am I to assume that she was with you all night?"

Clay watched Flynt ease a step closer to the truck, his eyes narrowed in suspicion.

"Yes, sir," he said into the receiver, but kept a watchful eye on Flynt's expression before saying more. He debated his chances of rolling up the window and locking the door before Flynt threw the first punch. Flynt was Fiona's older brother, after all, and a protective one at that, if the rumors he'd heard about their relationship were true. "We drove to Mexico last night and got married."

Clay watched Flynt's eyes round, then narrow to thin slits.

"Good," Ford snapped. "Now *you* can worry about her. I'm through."

There was a click and the phone went dead. Clay returned it to Flynt.

"Do you want an explanation?" he asked Flynt. "Or do you want to just go ahead and beat the crap out of me?"

Flynt closed his hands over the open window and

squeezed until his knuckles turned white, an obvious attempt at self-control. "You eloped with my sister?"

Clay nodded.

"Were you drunk?"

"No."

"Was she?"

Clay snorted a laugh, but shook his head. "No. We were both sober."

His eyes still narrowed dangerously, Flynt flexed his fingers on the open window, as if anxious to take that punch. "Is she pregnant?"

That question caught Clay off guard. "No," he said quickly, then added more cautiously, "at least, I don't think she is."

Flynt flexed his fingers again, his gaze fixed on Clay. After a moment he dragged his hands from the window and took a step back. "You better be good to her," he warned, "or you'll have me to answer to."

Clay jerked his chin in acknowledgment of the warning as he put the gearshift into Reverse. "I'm no wife beater, if that's what you're worried about."

"It's not her physical safety I'm worried about," Flynt replied. "It's her heart that concerns me."

Fiona slipped her feet into her sandals, taking a moment to admire the candy-apple shade of red Lucille had painted her toenails. With a laugh of delight, she rose and headed for the reception desk out front, energized after her day at the spa.

"All done?" Ginger asked as Fiona approached the desk.

"Yes, and I feel like a new woman, thanks to Body Perfect's talented staff."

"We aim to please," Ginger replied as she flipped through the day's invoices, searching for Fiona's.

"Add thirty percent to the total, please," Fiona said, feeling generous. "Everyone was so kind to work me in."

Ginger made the notation at the bottom of the slip. "Do you want me to put this on your father's account?" she asked.

"Yes. Please."

Ginger pulled the keyboard in front of her and typed the information into the computer. Her brow wrinkled, as she studied the screen that popped up.

"Problem?" Fiona asked.

"I don't know," Ginger said. "I typed in your number correctly, I'm sure, but the computer won't let me access your father's account."

Dread rushed through Fiona, leaving her palms damp and her stomach queasy. Surely her father hadn't already made good his threat, she thought wildly. She pasted on a smile to hide her fears and plucked a platinum card from her purse. "Must be a glitch in the system." She passed the card to Ginger. "Just put it on this."

Holding her breath, she watched Ginger slide the

credit card through the machine, praying that her father hadn't had time to cancel her cards, as well.

Ginger passed the card back to Fiona, but kept her gaze averted, as if embarrassed. "I'm sorry, Fiona, but your credit card was refused."

Mortified, Fiona searched her mind for some way to explain this humiliating circumstance. She thumped her palm against her forehead. "Silly me," she said, laughing. "Of course, it was denied! I canceled the card this morning when I ordered a replacement with my married name on it."

Ginger looked at her then, her jaw sagging. "You got married? To who?"

Fiona laughed again, pleased that she'd thought of such a plausible explanation so quickly. "Clay Martin."

"Clay Martin?" Ginger repeated, obviously shocked.

"Yes. Clay Martin."

"Oh, my God!" Ginger exclaimed, placing a hand over her heart. "You lucky dog. That man is to die for!"

Irritated that Ginger thought *she* was the lucky one in the union, rather than Clay, Fiona had to work to keep her smile in place. "Aren't I, though," she replied sweetly. She plucked the invoice from the desk. "If it's all right with you, I'll just drop by tomorrow morning and take care of this little bill."

"No problem."

Fiona turned to leave, but stopped when Ginger called her name.

"Yes?" she said.

Ginger offered her an apologetic smile. "I'm sorry, Fiona. I was so surprised by your announcement that I forgot to offer my congratulations. I hope you and Clay will be very happy together."

It was all Fiona could do to keep from throwing up. "Why, thank you, Ginger," she said, with a politeness her mother would be proud of. "I'm sure we will be."

Four

On the drive back to the ranch that afternoon, Clay recalled Flynt's last words to him that morning.

It's her heart that concerns me.

Heart? Clay thought, snorting a laugh. He wasn't sure Fiona even had one. She *was* capable of breaking them, though. He'd heard stories of her escapades for years, and if what he'd heard was correct, her record as a love-'em-and-leave-'em kind of gal trailed all the way back to her junior-high days, when girls and boys first discovered the opposite sex.

Some attributed her fickleness to the fact that she was an identical twin, claiming her sister, Cara, had received all the good genes, leaving Fiona with all the bad. Whether or not the gene pool was to blame, Clay wasn't sure, but there was definitely a startling difference between the two sisters' personalities. Cara was known for her kindness, sweetness and nurturing spirit, while Fiona was heralded as a selfish, conniving, coldhearted tease, the classic "rich bitch."

And wasn't that just his luck, Clay thought grimly. He'd married the evil twin.

He made the turn into the drive that led to his house and spotted Fiona's Mercedes parked by the back door. Accustomed to coming home to an empty house, he felt odd knowing that someone was inside, awaiting his arrival. Unsure if he liked the feeling or not, he climbed down from his truck and headed inside.

As he reached the back porch, the door flew open and Fiona stormed out.

"Where have you been?" she demanded furiously.

He drew back in puzzlement. "I told you I'd be home at six." He glanced at his watch. "It's only five after. What's the big deal?"

She spun back into the house, then whirled to face him when he followed her inside, her face red with fury. "I'll tell you what the big deal is! I couldn't pay my spa bill. Daddy blocked my access to his country-club account and canceled my credit cards."

Clay wrinkled his brow, trying to find the crisis in that announcement. "So?"

She balled her hands into fists at her sides. "So!" she screeched loudly enough to make his ears bleed. "Is that all you can say is *so?* I was humiliated! Mortified! If you could have seen Ginger's pitying look when she told me my credit card had been denied." She covered her face with her hands, as if the image alone was too much for her to bear. "I'll never be able to show my face at the country club again," she wailed. "Never!"

Not at all clear about what was going on, Clay took her by the elbow and guided her to the table. Easing her down onto a chair, he dragged up another and sat down in front of her. "Maybe you better start at the beginning and tell me what happened."

She dropped her hands to fist them in her lap, her eyes dark with accusation. "It's all your fault! If you'd given me money this morning when I asked, none of this would have happened."

Clay pushed back in his chair as if to distance himself from the blame. "Now wait just a damn minute. I gave you money."

"Twenty measly dollars? That wasn't even enough to cover my tips!"

"Maybe you should have thought about that before you ran up a big bill."

"I *did* think about it," she all but screamed. "But it never occurred to me that Daddy would've had time to make good his threats."

"Threats?" Clay repeated. "What threats?"

She covered her face again and bent double, moaning.

"Fiona?" he prodded. "What threats?"

She lifted her head, her eyes swimming with tears. "He told me he was going to close my bank account and cancel my credit cards."

"And knowing that, you tried to use them, anyway?"

"Well, of course I did! I couldn't just walk out of the spa without paying!"

"So how did you pay?"

She shot to her feet, her knees knocking against his, her eyes wild. "That's just it! I couldn't! I had to promise Ginger I'd return tomorrow morning and take care of my bill, which means I'll have to suffer the humiliation all over again.''

"And how do you plan to get your hands on the money between now and morning?''

She sniffed. "My monthly allowance. Daddy said he was going to deposit it into your account.''

Carson hadn't mentioned that little detail to Clay. "How much does he usually give you?''

"Two thousand dollars.''

"A month?'' he asked, shocked by the amount.

"Yes. A month.''

"Do you have to pay any bills with that money?''

She shook her head. "No. Daddy pays all my bills—or he did,'' she added, tears filling her eyes again.

Clay puffed his cheeks and blew out a long breath. He certainly had his work cut out for him, no question about that. And it looked as if the lessons in responsibility he'd agreed to teach Fiona were going to start sooner than he'd anticipated.

Catching her hand, he pulled her back down to the chair. "Daddy's not paying your bills anymore,'' he informed her.

Her chin quivered. "I know.''

He dragged a pad from the table and propped it on his crossed knee. "The first thing we need to do is establish a budget.''

"A budget?''

Sighing, he drew a pen from his shirt pocket. "Yes,

a budget.'' He held the pen poised above the paper. ''What are your fixed monthly expenses?''

She looked at him blankly.

''You know. Housing, transportation, food, fuel— stuff like that.''

She shook her head. ''I live at home. Or, rather, I *used* to live at home,'' she amended, her chin trembling again. ''So I don't have any housing expenses. I paid cash for my car, so—''

''Your *daddy* paid cash for your car,'' he reminded her.

She pursed her lips. ''Okay, so Daddy paid for my car. But the bottom line is, I don't have a car payment. And since I always ate my meals with my family, I didn't have any food expenses, either.''

Clay reared back in his chair and looked at her in disbelief. ''You're telling me that your father gives you two thousand dollars a month just to blow?''

She lifted her chin. ''Well, I wouldn't call it blowing, but yes, that's the amount I receive.''

Clay tossed the pad and pen to the table. ''Okay,'' he said, dragging his hands down his face. ''So how much do you owe the spa?''

She reached for her handbag, which was sitting on the table and pulled out the invoice to verify the total. ''Four hundred seventy-eight dollars and twenty-nine cents.''

His eyes shot wide at the amount. ''What did you do? Get a face-lift?''

Glaring at him, she stuffed the invoice back into her

purse. "I had the works," she informed him coldly, "which, for your information, is a massage, a manicure, a pedicure and a herbal seaweed wrap. Plus, I had lunch delivered from the Empire Room."

"*That* totaled up to almost five hundred dollars?"

"After the tip."

"Tip?"

"Yes, I had Ginger include a thirty percent gratuity."

"A thirty percent tip," he repeated. He stood, dragging a hand over his hair. "Man, I'm in the wrong business."

He pulled out his wallet and tossed a twenty and a one onto the table, then dug in his pocket and counted out seventy-one cents in change and dropped it on top of the bills.

Fiona shifted her gaze from the miserly pile to peer at Clay in confusion. "What's this for?"

He looked down his nose at her. "That, my dear, is what's left of your weekly allowance."

"But what about my bill at the spa?" she cried in alarm.

"I'll take care of it myself first thing in the morning. On second thought," he said, and reached to pull the twenty from the bottom of the stack. "*That's* what's left of your allowance," he said, indicating the dwindling pile. "I forgot that I gave you a twenty this morning."

Having spent a sleepless night, Fiona lay on the bare lumpy mattress, her throat clogged with tears. She heard the slam of the back door, and knew that was the sound of Clay leaving for work. He was mean, she told herself. Cruel. How did he expect her to exist for a whole week on $1.71? It was impossible! Ludicrous!

Especially since she no longer had her credit cards or her daddy's bank account to fall back on.

She stuck a finger between her teeth and bit it, refusing to give in to the tears. She wouldn't cry, she told herself. And she wouldn't beg, either. If this was a game her father and Clay Martin had devised to turn her into a sniveling, submissive woman, they were both in for a huge surprise. She'd die before she'd ask either one of them for a dime.

In spite of the pain she inflicted on her finger, the tears pushed higher. Oh, God, she sobbed silently. She was poor! All but destitute! Here she was, *the* Fiona Carson, her luxurious lifestyle, her very existence whittled down to a bare mattress in a tastelessly decorated bedroom in an equally gauche house, stuck out on a rundown ranch miles from town.

Without money, where could she go? What could she do? How would she pass the time? Her gas tank registered dangerously close to empty, a circumstance she'd tried to remedy on the way home from the spa the afternoon before. But when she'd swiped her card through the pay-at-the-pump device at the service station, the machine had refused the charge. Her father had even canceled her oil company cards!

Feeling her panic rising, she caught herself just

short of screaming and tearing at her hair and made herself draw three slow, deep breaths. She could do this, she told herself. She wasn't some weak-kneed female who had to depend on a man for her existence, her happiness. She was strong, healthy, intelligent. It was just a matter of thinking through her problems and finding workable solutions.

She sat up and scooted from the bed. She'd take a bubble bath, she told herself, as she headed for the bathroom. A nice, long soak in the tub always calmed her, plus it would improve her perspective.

But a search through the bathroom cabinets for bath oils or salts, produced only a mildewed can of toilet bowl cleaner and an icky-looking plumber's helper. Determined not to let the lack of toiletries deprive her of a much-needed soak in the tub, she squared her shoulders and marched for the kitchen. She snatched the bottle of dishwashing liquid from the back of the sink, returned to the bathroom, twisted on the taps, then squirted a generous stream of soap beneath the water. Within seconds bubbles churned in the tub.

Congratulating herself on her cleverness, she quickly stripped off her clothes and stepped into the tub, purring her contentment as she slid chin-deep into the water. When she climbed out an hour later, her skin the wrinkled texture of a dried prune, she felt calmer, much more capable of handling her problems. Toweling off, she glanced at the pile of clothes she'd dropped to the floor and curled her nose. She would *not* put those rags back on, she told herself, eyeing with distaste the black tank and capris that she'd literally been forced to wear twenty-four hours a day since her date with Roger. But what other choice did she have?

Arching a brow, she wrapped the towel around her and headed for Clay's room. She experienced only a slight pang of guilt as she entered his bedroom, but resolved it by telling herself that, since it was his fault she didn't have any clean clothes to wear, he certainly had no right to complain about her borrowing an item or two from his wardrobe.

But as she stepped inside, she slowed, startled by the starkness of the room. The walls were painted the same dreary, uninspired beige as the room he'd stuck her in, and the same cream-colored miniblinds, grayed by a thick layer of dust, covered the windows. Tangled across a king-size bed were jet-black sheets and a quilt that appeared homemade and faded from years of use. On an adjacent wall stood a long oak dresser.

Her attention captured by a picture propped on the corner, she crossed to the dresser. Frowning, she picked it up and moved to the window for a better look. Framed within the rectangle of dull pewter was a snapshot of Clay's family: his father and his mother in the middle, and Clay and his sister, Joanna, at either of their sides. Though the picture was years old—at least seven or eight, Fiona decided, judging by the style of the women's clothing and hair—she recognized Clay immediately.

Clutching the towel between her breasts to hold it

in place, she sat down on the edge of the bed to study the photo more closely. The picture was taken just before Clay had shipped out for overseas duty, she guessed, since he was dressed in his army uniform. His hair was sheared short, painfully so, his scalp white beneath the strict military haircut. But it was his face that held her attention—or rather his expression did. He looked bored, impatient, as if anxious to have the picture taken so he could be on his way.

But she saw bitterness there, as well.

Resting the picture on her lap, she lifted her head and stared out the window, trying to think back to that time. He would have been about twenty-two, maybe twenty-three, when he'd enlisted in the army. Her frown deepened as she tried to recall the circumstances behind his enlistment. Her brow smoothed as she remembered both the situation and the cause for his bitterness. Valerie's murder, she thought. That was it. Clay had enlisted shortly after the murder charges against him were dropped.

Was that the reason for his bitterness? she wondered, glancing back at the photo. If so, she could certainly understand not only his bitterness, but his impatience to leave Mission Creek behind.

So why had he returned? She frowned again as she puzzled over that oddity. What with the town's animosity toward him before his departure, and his parents both being deceased, what could possibly have drawn him back to Mission Creek?

Giving herself a shake, she rose and replaced the

picture. Whatever the reason, she told herself, he was back and doing his best to make her life miserable.

Reminded of his less-than-compassionate response to her restricted finances, she snatched open a drawer and began digging through its contents, searching for something of his to wear.

She pulled out a drab, olive-green T-shirt, shuddered at the army insignia emblazoned across its front, then dug around some more until she found a lightweight pair of sweatpants to complete the outfit. Dropping the towel, she dragged the T-shirt over her head, then stepped into the pants and drew the drawstring tight around her waist. She straightened and looked at her reflection in the dresser mirror…and shuddered.

"It's clean," she told herself, and turned away from her unflattering reflection. Besides, who would see her? With no gas in her car and no money to fill the tank, it appeared she was stuck in Nowhereville until she could either persuade Clay to give her an advance on her allowance or her fairy godmother showed up.

Personally she was betting on the fairy godmother. She figured her chances of squeezing even one red cent out of Clay ranked somewhere between slim and none.

Clay looked at the account balance listed at the bottom of his ATM receipt, rubbed his eyes to clear his vision, then looked again. Damn, he thought a little shakily, as he stared at the six-figure amount printed there. He'd never had that much money in his bank account at one time in his entire life.

Which could only mean Carson had kept his word and deposited not just the first installment of the amount he'd agreed to pay Clay once he and Fiona were married, but the second installment, as well.

Releasing his breath on a low whistle, he tucked the receipt into his wallet, then steered his truck out of the bank and onto the street, already thinking of all the things the money would buy. Fertilizer and seed to improve his pastures. The fencing supplies he needed to make the pastures secure for cattle again. Twenty or more heifers and a bull to service them. A stock trailer to haul the animals. Paint for the barn and tin to repair the roof. A squeeze chute to use when working the cattle.

But the first expense he had to cover, he reminded himself, was Fiona's debt at the country club, which was why he'd stopped at the bank in the first place. He shook his head, reminded of the astronomical amount she'd charged. Hell! he thought irritably. Entire families lived for a month on less than what she'd selfishly spent during one frivolous day at the spa.

Carson was right, he told himself. Fiona was totally irresponsible. The woman didn't have a clue about the value of money or what it took to earn it. But she'd learn, he promised himself. Carson had upheld his end of the bargain, and Clay was sure as hell going to uphold his.

Resolved to his fate, he pulled his truck into a parking space at the country club and climbed out.

"Body Perfect," he muttered under his breath, pushing open the frosted glass door to the spa. Wonder what marketing genius had come up with the name, one that was sure to make a woman bite. There wasn't a female alive who didn't yearn for the perfect body. Few ever realized their dream.

Ginger glanced up as he stepped inside.

"Well, hello, Clay," she said in surprise, then bit back a smile. "What can we do for you today? A facial? A pedicure?"

Clay shuddered at the very thought. "No, ma'am. I'm just here to pay Fiona's bill."

She stood as she accepted the cash he offered her. "I hear congratulations are in order."

"Congratulations?" he repeated.

She rang up the sale, laughing at his confused look. "Your marriage, silly. Fiona told me about it yesterday."

"Oh…yeah…our marriage." Clay felt the heat rising to his cheeks. "Thanks."

She gave him a curious look as she counted out his change. "Rather sudden, wasn't it?"

He quickly pocketed the money. "Yes, ma'am, it was." He tipped his hat in farewell, anxious to get out of there before she asked him any more questions he didn't know how to answer. "I better get on down the road. See you later."

He was out the door before she had a chance to

question him further. Once he made it to the parking lot, he stopped and released a shaky breath. That was a close one, he thought. And before he found himself faced with another situation in which he was expected to respond to questions about his marriage, he intended to nail down a few details with the parties involved. He'd start with Carson, he decided, get their stories straight, then confirm it all with Fiona later.

He made a detour around his truck and headed for the Men's Grill, figuring that was as good a place as any to find Carson at this time of day. Ford and his cronies usually huddled up there both before and after their morning round of golf. Personally Clay had never seen the man swing a club, but figured a golf game was a good excuse to get Ford out of the house and out from under his wife's watchful eye. Everyone in town knew Ford had a bad heart and a fondness for cigars and liquor, which Grace Carson was known to monitor like a hawk.

Sure enough, he found Ford in the grill, sitting with three of his buddies at a table near the door. Not wanting to discuss his business in front of the other men, Clay caught Carson's eye and signaled him to join him at the bar.

He settled on a stool and ordered a cup of coffee, watching Carson's reflection in the mirror behind the bar as he excused himself from the group.

Carson slid onto the stool next to his. "Mornin', son," he said, giving Clay an exuberant clap on the back. "Don't tell me you're already wantin' to throw in the towel."

Relieved to find that Carson wasn't still angry, Clay snorted a laugh and shook his head. "No, sir. Not yet."

"How are things going? You and Fiona gettin' along all right?"

Clay felt a stab of guilt, remembering his discussion with Fiona the previous night concerning her spending habits. "We're doing okay," he replied vaguely.

"Good. Good. I deposited the money into your account."

Clay nodded. "Yes, sir. I noticed that you did. And that's what I wanted to talk to you about," he added, lowering his voice so as not to be overheard. "Specifically the details of our arrangement. Fiona told one of the girls at the spa about the marriage. And you know how women like to talk. Before long, everybody in town is going to hear about it and start asking questions."

"Questions?" Ford repeated in confusion.

"Not questions so much as comments. Like how unexpected it was, what a surprise. That kind of thing. I need to know how you want me to respond."

Ford shrugged. "I'd say that's for you and Fiona to decide, not me. I'll go along with whatever the two of you agree on."

A little after noon Clay was able to squeeze some time out of his schedule to run out to the ranch to discuss with Fiona the best way to handle questions concerning their marriage.

But when he entered the house, he stopped cold two steps inside the door. He blinked once, then again, unsure he was seeing what he thought he was seeing. Sure enough, it was Fiona who lay sprawled on the sofa, one bare foot on the floor, the other hooked over the sofa's back, her eyes glued to the television set. She had a sack of microwave popcorn propped on her stomach and a half-empty bottle of beer cradled between her breasts. Two more bottles lay empty on the floor. Cookies spilled out of the open end of a bag of Oreos. Beside it lay a crumpled sack of potato chips.

"Fiona?"

When she didn't respond, he said more loudly, "Fiona!"

She tore her gaze from the screen to frown at him. "What?"

"Isn't it a little early in the day to be drinking beer?"

She gave the bottles on the floor a disinterested look, then returned her gaze to the television. "I was thirsty and that's all I could find to drink."

"You might have considered water," he said dryly. "You can get it fresh from the tap with very little effort."

"Shh!" she hissed, flapping a hand to silence him.

Hearing the screams and shouts coming from the television set, Clay stepped into the room so he could see the screen, certain some new tragedy had struck the world. But instead of finding the set tuned to a news report, he saw three women locked in a hair-pulling, nail-scratching wrestling match, while two thick-necked bouncers tried to separate them.

"What in hell are you watching?" he asked in dismay.

"Shh!" she hissed again. "It's a talk show. The two on the right are sisters. The chick on the left is their cousin. Supposedly the cousin's been sleeping with the redheaded sister's husband."

Clay couldn't have said what it was in her explanation that made him snap. Perhaps it was the hours he'd spent with the county medical examiner in the morgue that morning, reviewing the autopsy reports on a Jane Doe, whose badly decomposed body had been found by a local rancher. But whatever fueled his fury, he stalked across the room and angrily switched off the television.

"Hey!" Fiona struggled to sit up. "What did you do that for? They're about to bring out the husband and make him choose between the two women."

Balling his hands into fists at his sides in an effort to control himself, he turned to face her. "And you find that interesting?"

"Well, yes, as a matter of fact I do."

"Then you're as sick as they are. What's for lunch?"

She dropped back against the cushions in a pout. "I don't know. You tell me."

"You haven't cooked anything?"

She glanced down at the snacks scattered on the floor, then up at him. "That was all I could find to eat."

He braced his hands on his hips. "What the hell have you been doing all morning? Lying around watching TV and drinking beer?"

She curled her fingers around the bottle as if considering throwing it at him. "As I said, I couldn't find anything else."

"And I suppose it would've been too much trouble for you to go to the store and buy some groceries?"

"With *what?*" she returned acidly. "*You're* the one with all the money."

Afraid if he stayed a moment longer in the room with her he'd say something he'd regret, he turned to leave, but tripped over one of the beer bottles she'd discarded. He gave the bottle an angry kick that sent it spinning across the floor. The sound of it smacking against the opposite wall echoed in the quiet room.

Bracing his hands on the door frame, he sucked in a breath through clenched teeth. "I'm going back to work," he said, his voice as tight as the grip he had on the door. "When I get back tonight, I expect you to have this damn mess cleaned up."

Without a backward glance, he dropped his hands and strode out the door.

Fiona cleaned up the mess—but not because Clay had ordered her to do so. She cleaned it up because her mother had taught her the importance of picking up after oneself when a guest in someone else's home. Even if the hosts had household staff, her mother had maintained that one should never burden the staff unnecessarily. She'd also taught her children to leave a monetary gift for the staff member who'd seen to their personal needs, as compensation for whatever additional work their stay might have added to the staff member's normal duties.

Though Fiona was married to Clay and technically the mistress of his home, she considered herself nothing more than a guest. Her current living arrangements weren't permanent. She intended to leave the moment she was able to prove to her father that she was capable of taking care of herself.

After double-checking that the den was in order once again, she headed straight for her room and locked herself inside.

She wasn't hiding, she told herself as she curled up on the unmade bed. And she wasn't sulking, either. She just didn't want to chance bumping into Clay should he return.

And who could blame her? she asked herself with a sniff. The man was mean to the bone and as bad-tempered as a horse with a burr under its saddle. Was it *her* fault that she'd had nothing to do all morning but watch television? Was it *her* fault that there was nothing in this miserable house to drink but beer? She'd done the best she could with what was available to her. Where was the crime in that?

Hearing the sound of an engine outside, she rolled

from the bed and to her feet. Lifting the blinds a crack, she peered outside. She frowned when she saw Clay's truck parked in front of the detached garage. As she watched, the nose of a tractor appeared in the open garage doorway, with Clay behind the wheel.

She stepped quickly to the side, not wanting him to see her, and watched as he climbed down from the ancient-looking machine. He pulled a rag from the back pocket of his khaki slacks, lifted the engine cover, then stuck his head inside, restricting her view of him to his backside. She pressed a hand to her throat, her mouth going dry. He may be mean and bad-tempered, she thought weakly, but he was built like a brick wall. Broad shoulders, narrow waist, a nicely rounded and muscled derriere.

She watched him poke around a bit at the engine, then pull something out. He dropped the cover back into place and took a step back.

Her breath shuddered out of her on a sigh as he turned. And a face that would make a woman beg, she added to the list of his good qualities, unable to tear her gaze away. The Roman nose, the chiseled features, those dark, almost black eyes.

Furious with herself for even noticing his features, much less finding them attractive, she dropped her hand from the blind and let it fall back into place.

Looks weren't everything, she told herself as she climbed back on the bed. She'd had her pick of the best-looking men the state of Texas had to offer and, after no longer than a week or two, she'd discovered flaws in them all. Clay Martin had his faults, too, she reminded herself.

And skinflint topped the list.

Five

By morning Fiona had come up with a plan.

She'd persuade Clay to convince her father that his fears about her inability to take care of herself were unfounded. Why she hadn't thought to enlist his aid before was beyond her.

It was brilliant!

And if Clay didn't see things her way? Well, she knew how to sway him. She might not understand the basics of establishing and maintaining a budget, but she definitely knew how to get what she wanted from a man. She'd honed her skills to a razor-sharp edge over the years, wrapping man after man around her little finger until she'd gotten what she wanted from each.

And she'd wrap Clay, too, she thought smugly. It was just a matter of setting her mind to the task.

Pleased with herself, she pushed herself up to her elbows—and had to lock her arms to keep from throwing the covers back over her head.

Oh, God, she thought, squeezing her eyes shut to block out the sight of the depressing beige walls. Until she was able to persuade Clay to help her put an end to this stupid marriage, *this* was the view she'd wake to every morning.

She opened her eyes, then narrowed them at the wall. But that didn't mean she couldn't do something to pump up the ambiance a little.

And she was starting right now.

Fiona pushed open the front door to her family home and stopped, clasping her hands together as she drank in the familiar sights and scents that rushed out to greet her. Home, she thought, blinking back a sudden swell of emotion. It was all she could do to keep from dropping to her knees and kissing the marble floor.

"Fiona?"

She whirled. "Anita!" she cried, and ran to throw herself into the housekeeper's arms. "Oh, my gosh, but I've missed you," she said, hugging the woman tightly.

Anita twisted free to wag a scolding finger in front of Fiona's nose. "You run away and get married without telling Anita, then dare to say you miss me? Ha!"

Fiona wrinkled her nose. "Who told you? Daddy?"

"The *señor?*" Anita humphed. "The *señor*, he tells me nothing. No one tells Anita anything. She must hear everything from strangers."

"Strangers?" Fiona repeated, wondering who could possibly know about her marriage.

"*Sí*. Strangers. At the market this morning, I hear two women talking about this marriage of yours."

"Ginger," Fiona said with a groan, having forgotten that she had mentioned the marriage to her.

"I do not know the women's names who gossip, only what I overhear them say, and that is that my *niña* married without telling her Anita."

Fiona gave the housekeeper another quick hug. Though Anita hadn't been working long for the Carsons, the two had become close. "I'm sorry. You should have heard it from me first."

"*Sí,*" Anita agreed, nodding, then planted her hands on her ample hips. "And what do you think your *madre* is going to say when she returns from her visit with your sister, Cara, and discovers that her daughter has eloped while she was away?"

Fiona winced, then shrugged off the guilt before it could settle on her. "Daddy can handle that one, since this silly marriage was his idea."

Seeing Anita's confused look, Fiona smiled and looped her arm through the housekeeper's. "Never mind. I need a favor," she said as she drew the woman with her toward her private suite of rooms in the Carson home. "I want you to show me how to make a bed."

The housekeeper stopped short to gape at Fiona. "Make a bed?" she repeated. "You?"

Fiona laughed at the housekeeper's shocked expression. "Yes, me. Will you teach me?"

"*Sí,*" Anita said. "But will you learn? *That* is the question."

"I'll learn," Fiona promised. She looped her arm

through Anita's again and walked with her into the suite of rooms. Once inside she stopped, emotion filling her throat again as she gazed around her sitting room, with its creamy-yellow walls and blue toile draperies. "Anita?"

Already busy stripping the comforter from the bed for the first lesson, Anita said, "*Sí,* Fiona?"

"Are any of the cowboys around today?"

"*Sí.* A few, maybe. Why you ask?"

"I may need their help later."

Anita turned to look at her in puzzlement, a pillow caught between her hands. "For what?"

Fiona crossed the room, catching her lower lip between her teeth to hide her smile. "Oh, nothing too major."

There were days when Clay wondered if the entire population of the world had been stripped of its moral and ethical values or if it was just the company he kept. Everywhere he turned it seemed he was faced with one atrocity after another, the details surrounding each more sordid and depraved than the ones before.

His current caseload consisted of a murder, in which a pedophile had kidnapped and brutally killed a child, a teenager strung out on drugs who'd bludgeoned his parents to death with a dull ax, a string of convenience-store robberies that covered half the state, stolen Mayan artifacts smuggled into the United States across the Texas/Mexico border. The list went on and on.

And that was without taking into consideration the cases he worked on *un*officially. He continued to assist in the search for the parents of the baby left on the Lone Star Country Club's ninth tee, worked in an advisory capacity on the rescue of a man held in a Central American prison by terrorists, plus offered his expertise on a number of other cases centered in and around Mission Creek.

More often than not, the minute he hit the front door at the end of a day, he headed straight for the shower, desperate to wash off the evil he was sure had rubbed off on him from the lowlifes he was forced to deal with all day.

Today was no different.

But when he entered his house, he only made it as far as the hallway before he was stopped cold. He turned slowly back around. That wasn't his chair, he thought in confusion, staring at the tobacco-colored leather club chair he'd just passed. And those weren't his pictures, he thought, his gaze going to the framed oil paintings hanging on the wall between the front windows. Hell, he didn't even own any art!

There was only one explanation.

"Fiona!"

"Back here!" she called.

The cheerfulness in her voice had his eyes narrowing to slits. He stalked down the hall toward her room. "Where the hell did all that crap in the den come from?"

"What crap?" came her muffled reply.

He stepped into her room and stopped, shocked by the room's altered state. Drapes flanked the once bare windows and pooled into soft gauzy puddles on the floor. The old double-bed frame and mattress that had been there had been replaced with a queen-size canopy bed covered with a thick, down-filled comforter and a mountain of decorative pillows of verifying shapes and textures. A sky-blue velvet chaise sat in front of the window, arranged to take advantage of the view. Against the opposite wall stood a massive mahogany armoire, its heavily carved doors thrown wide. Fiona sat in front of it, pulling clothes from a suitcase and tucking them into a drawer.

She glanced over her shoulder and beamed at him. "Hi. What crap?"

She'd gone shopping, was all he could think. She'd spent a fortune—probably *charged* a fortune—to buy all this stuff. And since her father had cut her off, he could only assume that she'd charged the purchases to him.

"It's going back," he said, barely able to control the rage that boiled inside him. "Do you understand? Every damn bit of this crap is going back where it came from."

Her forehead wrinkling in puzzlement, she tucked the sweater she held into the drawer, then stood. "But why?"

"Because we don't need it!" he shouted. "And I sure as hell can't afford it. I can barely make the notes on this place as it is."

Fiona stared at him, her plan to charm him into helping her forgotten. Setting her jaw, she took a step toward him. "I didn't buy this 'crap,' as you referred to it. It's mine. Every last bit of it."

He could only stare. "Yours?"

She jutted her chin. "Yes, mine. And I'm not hauling it all back home. I may have to live in this…this…" She fluttered her hands at the room, searching for the right word to describe it. It didn't take her long to come up with one. "This hovel," she said, with a shudder. "But that doesn't mean I can't have a few of my personal possessions around to make my stay here more pleasant, not to mention more comfortable."

Hovel? Clay thought, her description stabbing like a knife to the heart. Is that what she thought of the house he'd grown up in? The place he was struggling desperately to hold on to?

"Fine," he growled, then leveled a finger at her nose. "But you better make damn sure you don't throw out any of my stuff to make room for yours. If you do…"

Letting the threat dangle unfinished in the air between them, he turned and stalked from her room.

Clay stepped under the shower, letting the icy needles of water cool his temper. After five minutes beneath the punishing spray, he braced his hands on the tiled wall and dropped his chin to his chest with a weary sigh.

He shouldn't have yelled at her, he told himself. He should have asked questions before assuming the worst and jumping down her throat. Even if her reasons for doing so were insulting, she had every right to bring some of her own things into his home.

She deserved an apology, he told himself, though the thought of offering her one left a bitter taste in his mouth. But if nothing else, Clay was fair. When he was wrong, he owned up to his mistakes and was quick to set things right.

Twisting off the faucet, he dragged a towel from over the shower door and stepped out onto the worn linoleum floor. After drying off, he pulled on a pair of clean jeans, tugged a T-shirt over his head and headed for the hall.

At the doorway to Fiona's room, he paused and peeked inside. He found her sitting on the floor in front of the armoire, her head bent, her shoulders drooped, while she plucked at a nubby sweater she held on her lap. She looked miserable, beaten. The fact that Clay was responsible for her current depressed mood only added to his guilt. She wasn't any happier about this marriage than he was, he reminded himself. They were both helpless pawns in a game of chess her father had devised.

Promising himself to be more understanding, more patient, he took a step into the room. "Fiona?"

She snapped her shoulders back at the sound of his voice and quickly stuffed the sweater into a drawer.

"Unless you're here to offer an apology," she said tersely, "you can leave."

"I'm sorry."

She whipped her head around to stare at him, obviously not having expected him to offer her one.

With a wry smile, he crossed to her. "When I'm out of line, I usually realize it sooner or later."

She pressed her lips together and reached to snatch another article of clothing from the suitcase, avoiding his gaze. "You were definitely out of line in this instance."

He hunkered down beside her, bracing an arm on his thigh. "Forgive me?"

She gave her chin a haughty lift and yanked open a drawer, refusing to look at him. "I might."

He bit back a smile at her stubbornness. "Should I expect it in this lifetime?"

"Maybe."

He chuckled and sat down cross-legged beside her. "I guess that'll have to do."

"I guess it will," she replied with a sniff, "since that's the best you're getting from me."

While she continued to fuss with her clothes and ignore him, he looked around, noting the furniture and accessories she'd moved into the room, wondering how she'd managed to handle it all. That armoire alone had to weigh a good three or four hundred pounds. "How did you get all this stuff over here?" he asked.

"I didn't pay someone to move it, if that's what you're worried about."

Sure that he deserved the snide remark, he caught her hand and pulled her around to face him.

"I said I was sorry," he said quietly. "The question was an honest one and asked out of simple curiosity." He tipped his head, indicating the armoire. "That thing must weigh a ton."

Grimacing, she dropped her chin. "Trust me, it does."

"So who moved it? I know you couldn't have done it alone."

"Some of the cowboys from the ranch. And I didn't pay them," she was quick to inform him.

He arched a warning brow. "I think we've already established that no money changed hands. What I'd like to know is how you talked them into moving all this stuff for you."

She shrugged. "I just asked."

"You just asked," he repeated, then dropped back his head and laughed. From a woman like Fiona, he knew a simple request was all it would take to have a man tying himself in knots to fulfill it.

She pursed her lips. "What's so funny?"

He shook his head, still chuckling. "Nothing. I was just picturing all those cowboys sweating and straining, while you stood by filing your nails and issuing orders."

She snatched her hand from his, and he immediately regretted the thoughtless remark. His hand felt empty now, cold, without the softness and warmth of hers filling it.

"You make me sound like some kind of prima donna."

Anxious to avoid another shouting match, he caught her hand again and rose, pulling her to her feet, as well. "No. You're a woman who knows how to get what she wants."

She eyed him, as if unsure whether he'd meant that as a compliment or an insult.

Chuckling, he slung an arm around her shoulders and urged her toward the door. "What's for dinner? I'm starving."

"Dinner?" she repeated, peering up at him in alarm. "You expect *me* to cook?"

"Well, yeah," he said in surprise. "What else have you got to do all day?"

As soon as the words were out of his mouth, he knew they were the wrong ones. He quickly hauled her back against his side, before she could start pecking at him again, and aimed them both for the kitchen. "I've got sandwich makings in the refrigerator," he said, hoping to smooth her ruffled feathers. "We'll make do with a cold meal tonight."

Clay learned quickly that Fiona was a stranger to a kitchen. After watching her stare blankly into the refrigerator for a good five minutes, he guided her to a chair and made the sandwiches himself. While he was building them, he remembered that the day before he'd never gotten around to discussing with her what details of their marriage they would make public. Unsure how best to broach the subject without setting off another argument, he placed their plates on the table, then sat down opposite her.

He took a bite of his sandwich, then glanced over at her. "I saw your dad yesterday at the country club."

She stiffened at the mention of her father, then lifted an indifferent shoulder. "Lucky you."

He bit back a smile. The woman definitely knew how to hang on to a grudge. "Yeah, I thought it was rather a fortunate encounter myself. Probably saved me hours trying to track him down."

Poised for the first bite, she snapped her gaze to his. "What did you want to see my father about?"

"Wanted to straighten out a few things. I saw Ginger at the spa," he explained further. "She made a comment about our marriage being rather sudden, and I wasn't sure how to respond. I thought it might be wise to ask your father how much of our arrangement he wants to be made public before I find myself caught in that situation again."

Fiona laid down her sandwich, her appetite gone, as she imagined the townspeople's reaction when word got around that her father had *paid* Clay Martin to marry her. She'd be the laughingstock of Mission Creek!

"And what did he say?" she asked uneasily.

He lifted a shoulder. "He said he'd go along with whatever story we concocted."

Fiona found that only mildly reassuring, since she wasn't at all sure how far a man as honorable as Clay would be willing to stretch the truth. "So what explanation do you suggest we offer?"

He lifted a shoulder again. "Doesn't matter to me. I just think it's important that we're all reading from the same script."

"Good idea," she said, picking up her sandwich and trying her best to appear as unconcerned as he.

Frowning, she nibbled at the sandwich while she tried to think of a plausible explanation for their rushed marriage—one in which she didn't wind up looking like some hopeless spinster her father was desperate to pawn off on the first available man.

"We've been friends since we were children," she began, but stopped when Clay gave her a dubious look.

"Okay," she said irritably. "So maybe we weren't friends, but we at least knew each other." She took a sip of her milk, then stared off into space as she let the story build in her mind.

"You've been gone for years," she said, picking up the tale again. "So no one can question what kind of relationship we might have had while you were away. For all they know, we could've been corresponding by mail the whole time you were in the army."

"It's possible," he allowed.

"And through our correspondence, you fell hopelessly in love with me."

When he choked on his milk, she gave him a sour look. "Well, you could've."

Trying not to laugh, he waved a hand, urging her to go on with her story.

"We could tell everyone that you grew weary with all the danger and intrigue and wanted only to be with me, so you tossed aside a promising career in the military and rushed home to profess your love and propose."

He hooted a laugh at the ceiling. "You missed your calling, Fiona. You should have been a romance writer."

She ignored the interruption. "But I refused to marry you then, of course, because I didn't want to steal the spotlight from Cara."

"Steal the spotlight from Cara?"

"Well, yes," she said, surprised that he'd question her sensitivity to her twin sister's feelings. "It wouldn't have been fair if I'd announced my engagement with Cara having just announced her own. Everyone's attention would naturally have shifted to me."

"I see," Clay said, again trying his best not to laugh.

She set down her sandwich, doubt clouding her eyes. "They'll believe me, won't they?"

Realizing how important it was for her to save face, Clay reached across the table to cover her hand with his. "They'll believe whatever you want them to believe."

She closed her fingers around his, her grip almost desperate. "You really think so?"

He gave her hand a quick squeeze, then released it to pick up his glass of milk. "Fiona, if you told everyone that I'd kidnapped you and held a gun to your head, forcing you to repeat your vows, not a one of 'em would dare question the truth in your story."

"Kidnapped," she repeated, as if the idea of her being forced to marry held a certain appeal. Then she frowned and shook her head. "Although I like your version more, I think we'd better stick with mine. I wouldn't be able to live with the guilt."

Though Clay was sure he'd regret asking, curiosity got the better of him. "Guilt? For what?"

"You losing your job," she said, as if stating the obvious. "If it got around that you'd kidnapped me, the governor would jerk your badge for sure. No," she said, shaking her head again. "We'd better stick with my story."

Later that evening Clay backed his truck up to the barn and began unloading the fencing supplies he'd purchased in town earlier that day. With the money he'd received from Carson, he knew he could well afford to hire someone else to do the work, but he'd elected to do it himself. Granted, he'd save the cost of labor, but he'd based his decision on more than just money. He wanted to do the work, needed to. Sweat equity, his dad had always called it. For every ounce of sweat he put into making the improvements, he was investing that much more of himself into the place. He owed a debt to both the ranch and his parents, one he was determined to pay back.

He dragged a spool of barbed wire to the edge of the tailgate, then hefted it to his shoulder and turned for the barn. As he did, he chuckled, remembering the romantic tale Fiona had concocted to explain away whatever questions the unexpectedness of their marriage might spawn.

"Tossed aside a promising military career to be with her," he said, then laughed heartily as he heaved the spool of wire onto the worktable. The woman had an ego the size of Texas, but damn, if she wasn't entertaining to be around.

He couldn't remember the last time he'd laughed so hard, especially with a woman.

He turned again for the truck, but stopped, his gaze snagged by the house in the distance. His smile melted as he stared at the window of Fiona's room. The light was on and he could just make out her form between the blind's open slats. As he stared, he saw her cross her arms in front of her and pull her shirt up over her head. As she dropped her arms, she shook her hair back, the dark tresses cascading past her shoulders. A knot twisted low in his groin as he stared, mesmerized by the swell of her breasts beneath a lace bra. A vision of her the night he'd caught her skinny-dipping at the country club pushed into his brain. Water sluicing down her nude body, droplets glittering like diamonds at the tips of her breasts. The black lace thong that had clung wetly to her body, the thin strip of silk that had disappeared between the cheeks of her butt. The provocative sway of her hips as she'd walked away from him. The seductive gleam in her green eyes, the moist warmth of her breath as she'd turned in his arms and looked up at him.

As she reached for the waist of her shorts, he turned away, squeezing his eyes shut against the sight, the memory…the temptation. He wouldn't let her get to him, he told himself. Couldn't. He'd made the mistake of getting involved with one spoiled rich girl—and she'd ripped out his heart when she'd grown bored with him and moved on to another man, another challenge.

He wouldn't make the same mistake again.

The next morning Fiona was in the kitchen before Clay—her appearance there by design, not chance. His temper tantrum the afternoon before had sidetracked her from her plan to charm him into helping her. But today she intended to start fresh.

Hearing his footsteps in the hallway, she quickly fluffed her hair, gave the neckline of her teddy one last tug lower over her breasts, then wet her lips and struck a seductive pose.

"Good morning, Clay."

He glanced her way, frowned and made a fast detour for the refrigerator. "Mornin'."

She pursed her lips, irritated by his less-than-enthusiastic reaction to what she considered the sexiest lingerie in her wardrobe. Determined to have him eating out of her hand before he left the house, she pushed away from the counter and crossed to the refrigerator. She reached in front of him, purposely letting her breast brush his arm, and closed her fingers around a bottle of orange juice. Angling her face toward him, she smiled. "Sorry. I'll just get this and be out of your way."

Drawing the bottle of juice from the refrigerator, she turned toward him, rather than away, so that she now stood between him and the refrigerator. Sniffing the air, she rested a hand against his chest. "Oh, my. What cologne is that you're wearing?"

"I'm not. It's aftershave."

She rose on tiptoe and brushed her nose across his cheek. "Mmm," she hummed, as she sank back down to her heels. Tipping her face up to his, she curved her lips in a sensual smile and walked her fingers up his chest. "Well, whatever it is, you smell positively yummy."

She could tell that her plan was working. His neck had turned red just above his collar, and there was the tiniest little twitch at the corner of his eye, a sure sign that she was getting under his skin. She lifted her face and closed her eyes, sure that he was about to kiss her.

"I gotta go."

Her hand dropped from his chest, and she flipped open her eyes as he turned for the back door. She watched him grab his hat from the rack on the wall and pull it on.

Then the door slammed behind him and he was gone.

Fiona stood in front of the open refrigerator, the cold air wafting from it, making gooseflesh pop up on her bare arms.

Or was it the chill of rejection?

She narrowed her eyes at the sound of his truck engine revving. Okay, so maybe seduction wasn't the way to get what she wanted from him. But there were other methods, she told herself. One way or another she'd make him do what she wanted.

Fiona saw the service station just up ahead and glanced down at her fuel gauge. It registered below empty. She breathed a sigh of relief, sure that she'd made the last mile on fumes alone.

She steered her Mercedes into the bay closest to the convenience store and climbed out. As she did, she spotted a patrol car parked near the front door. "Harley-the-Bear," she murmured under her breath. "Oh, this is too perfect."

Assuming nonchalance, she strolled to the pump, pressed the button marked Pay Inside, then pulled out the nozzle. Smiling, she waved at the attendant who peered at her through the store's plate-glass window, then proceeded to fill her tank. When it was full, she replaced the nozzle and climbed back behind the wheel.

Laughing wildly, she stomped on the accelerator and shot out onto the highway, leaving a trail of rubber on the pavement behind her. With one eye on the rear-view mirror, she sped toward town.

Two miles short of the city-limit sign, she heard the wail of a siren. She glanced in the rearview mirror and saw the patrol car racing up behind her, red lights flashing. She drove a mile farther, just to make sure Harley was good and mad, then pulled to the shoulder, parked and waited. By the time he appeared at her window, his ears were red, his eyes bulging.

She pressed the lever to lower the glass. "Is there a problem, Officer?" she asked innocently.

"You know damn well and good there is, Fiona!" He waved a hand in the direction they'd come. "You drove off without paying for your gas, exceeded the speed limit by a good thirty miles an hour and ignored my signals for you to pull over." Clamping his lips together, he whipped out his citation pad. "You're getting a ticket this time, little lady. A big one. And after I write the ticket, I'm marching your butt right back down to that station and you're going to pay for that gas."

Fiona shoved open her door, cracking Harley in the knee with the door panel. "Now wait just a minute," she said, ignoring Harley's yelp of pain. "You can't write me a ticket."

He looked up at her, his lips curled in a snarl, while he rubbed his knee. "I damn sure can. And your daddy'll thank me for doing it, so don't go pulling that do-you-know-who-I-am crap with me. Ford and me go all the way back to high school, and I happen to know he's had a stomachful of your shenanigans, the same as me and everybody else in this town."

Her mouth dropped open, then closed with a click of teeth. "Well, we'll just see about that now, won't we?" She snatched the pad from his hand and ripped out the remaining forms and flung them in the air.

Harley's face turned purple with rage. With a low growl, he clamped a hand over her wrist and dragged her toward the patrol car.

"What are you doing?" Fiona cried, digging in her heels. "Where are you taking me?"

"To jail." He yanked open the back door and pointed a cigar-shaped finger at the back seat. "Get in."

With a sniff, Fiona slid onto the seat. So far, things were going exactly as she'd planned. "I'm entitled to a phone call," she reminded him as he climbed behind the wheel.

He shot her a glare in the rearview mirror. "You can call the president of the United States of America, for all I care. But you'll make the call at the station." He shoved the car into gear. "You're not wasting the taxpayers' good money burnin' up minutes on my cell phone. Nosiree," he said, shaking his head. "You'll make your call at the station, same as any other criminal."

Six

Hunkered down by a dry creek bed, Clay studied the parched ground, trying to re-create the murderer's movements in his mind. He knew the rancher had found the woman's body facedown, her hands tied behind her back, approximately ten feet from where Clay knelt. During the initial investigation, the police hadn't found tire marks of any kind within the area, so that meant that the murderer had arrived and left by foot. Clay rubbed his fingers over the dry ground, then sighed and drew his hand back to brush his fingers across his thigh. And they wouldn't be finding any footprints, either, he thought, frowning. The ground was so hard, a herd of buffalo could stampede across it and not leave a trail.

He closed his eyes and tried to force his mind to that of the murderer, think as he might have thought, get a feel for the path he might have taken. But the only image that came to mind was of Fiona, dressed in that scrap of nothing she'd had on that morning, her face tipped up to his, her lips full and moist, slightly parted, as if awaiting his kiss. He could almost feel the heat of her body surging against his, the imprint of each of her fingers on his chest.

With a groan, he squeezed the bridge of his nose and tried to blank out the image. He wouldn't let her get to him, he told himself. He couldn't. She was toying with him. Why, he wasn't sure, but she was definitely trying to mess with his mind.

He'd known from the moment he stepped into the kitchen that she was up to something. She was never awake when he left for work, and he seriously doubted that the purpose behind all that bumping and grinding in front of the refrigerator was due to a thirst for orange juice. She'd had seduction on her mind.

And she'd come damn close to achieving her goal.

Even now, he could feel the silky brush of her skin across his cheek, see the expectancy and warmth in the eyes she'd lifted to his, smell her sensual fragrance wafting beneath his nose. He'd come within a hairsbreadth of kissing her. And he knew if he had, he wouldn't have been able to stop with a kiss. He'd have wound up carrying her to his bed and making love to her.

Fortunately sanity had returned before he succumbed to temptation.

Swearing, he surged to his feet. He wouldn't let her get to him, he told himself. She was trouble with a capital T.

He turned in a slow circle, forcing his mind from thoughts of Fiona and back to the investigation, to the job at hand. He centered his attention on establishing the direction the murderer might've taken, either in coming or going. To the north lay a state highway. To the east, another larger ranch butted up against the boundaries of the one where the body had been found. To the west was the rancher's home. South…

He turned to face that direction and started walking. If he remembered correctly, the land to the south was used strictly for hunting. Thousands of acres of nothing but deep thickets of trees and overgrown vegetation, the perfect cover for wildlife…or a murderer. There were a couple of cabins there, too, as he recalled. Crude, one-room structures hunters used during deer season.

Playing a hunch, Clay ducked between the strands of barbed wire fencing that separated one ranch from the other and continued on, keeping his eyes on the ground. He crossed the bed of the dry creek, climbed the opposite bank and looked back. He narrowed his eyes, searching for anything out of the ordinary, something that would offer a clue to the identity of the murderer, the woman murdered or the path that had led to her death. He shifted his gaze, then looked back quickly, sure that he'd caught a flicker of light in his peripheral vision. The sun striking a piece of metal or glass? he wondered. Maybe. He started down the bank, keeping his eyes fixed on the spot where he thought he'd seen the glancing light.

In the bed of the dry creek, he stopped and knelt, running his hand over the dry, brittle stubs of grass that grew there. On the second sweep, he caught a glimpse of metal. Carefully he spread the blades of grass. A silver disk the size of a quarter caught the sunlight and reflected it back at his eyes. Holding the grass aside, he reached in his back pocket and pulled out his handkerchief. Spreading it over the disk, he gently lifted it, taking care not to contaminate the evidence, if that was what it proved to be.

He stood and folded back the edges of his handkerchief to study the piece of metal more closely. "I'll be damned," he murmured, noting the engraved medical insignia that designated the wearer as a diabetic. "Looks as if our Jane Doe might finally have a name."

His cell phone rang, startling him. He quickly folded the handkerchief back over the medallion and slipped it into his shirt pocket, then reached for his phone.

"Martin," he said into the receiver.

The only sound he heard was a woman's hysterical crying.

He tensed, holding the phone closer to his ear. "Fiona?"

"Oh, Clay," she sobbed. "You've got to come and get me."

He took off at a run, his heart pounding, the phone clutched to his ear. "Where are you? Are you hurt?"

"No," she wailed. "I'm in jail!"

Clay couldn't ever remember being angrier—or more embarrassed—in his entire life. His own wife, for God's sake, thrown in jail.

As he strode into the police station, Fiona rose from

a chair beside a desk, stretching out her arms to him, her face streaked with tears. He ignored her and turned to the patrolman who stood nearby. "What happened, Harley?"

As the patrolman recounted the events that had led to her arrest, Clay's blood pumped hotter and hotter. Setting his jaw, he said, "I'll be right back."

"But, Clay—"

He shrugged off Fiona's hand as she grabbed for him and strode for the detective's office at the end of the long hall. He walked in without knocking and pulled the handkerchief from his pocket. "I think I have something you can use to trace down the identity of our Jane Doe." He tossed the wadded handkerchief onto the desk.

The detective glanced from it to Clay, then stood, using a pen to push aside the fabric. "Well, I'll be damned," he murmured, staring at the medallion.

"My sentiments exactly," Clay replied. "I found it lying in the creek bed on the hunting reserve south of the ranch where the body was found. You might want to check out some of the cabins there for more evidence. The murderer might have held her there for a while before he killed her."

The detective nodded. "Thanks, Clay. I owe you one."

"Find the murderer. That'll be thanks enough." He turned and headed back out the door.

Once in the control center again, he caught Harley's

eye and jerked his head, indicating for Harley to join him at the counter.

"How much are her fines?"

Harley named the amount and Clay pulled out his wallet. After counting out the cash, he shoved his wallet back into his hip pocket and stuck out his hand. "Sorry for the trouble, Harley," he said, and shook the patrolman's hand.

"You don't have anything to apologize for, Clay," Harley assured him, then turned to scowl at Fiona who had moved to stand behind Clay. "*She,* on the other hand, could spend the rest of her life apologizing for the trouble she's caused and not get done."

Fiona made a face at the patrolman, then quickly smoothed her expression to a soulful one when Clay glanced over his shoulder at her.

Frowning, he turned and caught her by the arm. "Let's get out of here."

She had to run to keep up with his angry stride.

Once inside the truck, he gripped the steering wheel and fixed his gaze on the windshield. "You may have gotten away with these childish pranks with your father," he said, barely able to control his rage, "but I'll be damned if I'll put up with your shenanigans."

Fiona's chin jutted out. She refused to let his anger intimidate her. "I needed gas."

He balled his hand into a fist and slammed it against the steering wheel, making her jump.

"Dammit, Fiona! That's the stupidest, most selfish

excuse I've ever heard for breaking the law, and believe me, I've heard them all.''

"Well, if you'd given me some money—"

"I *gave* you money," he shouted, "and you blew it all in one trip to the spa!"

"Yes, but that was before I knew that Daddy had cut me off.''

Clay ground his teeth, trying to get a grip on his anger. When he was sure he had, he yanked the gearshift into Reverse and backed out of the parking space.

"Are we going home?" she asked.

"No. I'm taking you back to the gas station."

"The gas station?" she repeated. "But why?"

"So you can pay for the gas you stole."

"Oh, please," she said, rolling her eyes. "You don't really expect me to go back there, do you?"

"I damn sure do."

She stared at his profile, then gulped, realizing by the determined set of his jaw that he was serious. "But couldn't you just stop by and pay for it after you drop me by the house?" she suggested hopefully.

"You're the one who stole. You're the one who'll pay."

Fiona slid down in the seat, squeezing her hands between her knees, and stared at the road ahead, suddenly feeling ill. No one had ever made her do anything like this before. Never. In the past when she'd done something crazy and impulsive, her daddy had always taken care of whatever mess she'd made. She'd never had to deal with the fallout from her pranks. Never!

Clay pulled up in front of the gas station, shoved the gearshift into Park. Through the plate-glass window, she could just make out the shape of the attendant. A low moan slipped past her lips.

Lifting a hip, Clay pulled out his wallet and tossed a twenty to her. She curled her fingers around the bill, swallowed hard, then opened her door.

Once inside, she glanced around and saw several customers milling the aisles. Hoping to pay for the gas and leave before they'd selected their purchases, she approached the counter. The attendant stood on the opposite side, slouched against a cigarette display rack while he thumbed through a *Playboy* magazine. "Excuse me," she said.

He turned his head, then jerked upright. "Hey! You're the lady who skipped without paying for your gas."

She winced, sure that everyone in the store had heard him and was now aware of her crime. "Yes," she murmured, feeling the heat crawl up her neck. "I came back to pay for it."

He braced his hands on the counter and leaned toward her. He had arms like Popeye and a tattoo of a bare-chested hula dancer that stretched from shoulder to wrist. As she stared, he flexed his muscle, and the dancer's hips swayed provocatively. She shuddered and dropped her gaze.

"Harley catch you?"

She gulped, nodded.

"Bet he slapped you with a pretty hefty fine, didn't he?"

She nodded again, sure that she felt the gaze of every customer in the store on her back. Desperate to escape the humiliation, she slid the twenty-dollar bill Clay had given her onto the counter. "This ought to cover the cost of the gas."

He let his gaze drop to her breasts, then looked back up at her and smiled, exposing a gold front tooth. He pushed the bill back across the counter and leaned closer. "How 'bout you work off that debt, instead?" he suggested in a low voice. "I bet a woman like you is hell in bed."

She snapped her head up, her eyes wide with shock. She felt a hand settle low on her back and turned to see that Clay had entered the store and moved to stand beside her.

"Is there a problem?" he asked the attendant.

Though his tone was friendly, Fiona saw the threat that darkened his eyes.

The attendant lifted his hands from the counter and took a step back. "No. No problem." He snatched up the twenty, rang up the sale and pitched some change onto the counter.

Clay scraped the coins onto his palm, then stuffed them into his pocket. "Appreciate your understanding," he said, then tipped his hat and drew Fiona toward the door.

* * *

Fiona stood on the front porch, her arms wrapped around her waist, watching Clay drive away. He hadn't said a word to her after leaving the gas station, had barely given her time to climb down from the truck before he'd taken off again.

She wanted to hate him for not responding as she'd thought he should to her arrest, but she couldn't seem to work up the venom required for the emotion. She'd thought he would storm into the police station, as her daddy always had, give the officer who'd arrested her a piece of his mind, then tuck her protectively under his arm, take her home and spend the rest of the day coddling her, trying to make up for whatever trauma she had suffered from the experience.

But he hadn't done any of those things. Oh, he'd stormed, all right. But his anger had been directed at *her,* not at the arresting officer. He'd made her feel small. Petty. Spoiled. That alone should have made her angry with him. But it didn't.

But she felt something else, too, besides pettiness. A small bubble of emotion that had lodged itself in her throat at the gas station when she'd felt the reassuring warmth of his hand on her back and looked up to find him at her side.

Gratitude? Yes, definitely. From the moment he'd told her she had to go back and pay for the gas, she'd been terrified at the thought of having to face the attendant alone. She had been grateful for Clay's presence, especially after the attendant's crude suggestion.

But it was more than gratitude she'd felt. It was… what?

Unable to name the emotion, with a sigh she turned and went inside.

Clay knocked on the door marked Private, then shuffled his feet uneasily while he waited for a response. Hearing a muffled "Come on in," he eased the door open and peered inside. Flynt sat behind a massive mahogany desk, his back to the door, his gaze on a computer screen in front of him.

Flynt glanced over his shoulder. "Hey, Clay," he said, smiling. "Give me a sec to shoot off this e-mail and I'll be right with you."

Clay dragged off his hat and crossed the room. He sat down in a leather wing chair opposite the desk and hooked his hat over his knee.

Flynt closed the screen, spun around and pulled the chair back to the desk. "Your timing couldn't be better. I just heard from Tyler. He said to tell you thanks for the lead. Appears that friend of yours in Central America is going to be a big help. Seems the place where Westin's being held captive is only about a hundred miles from where Tyler landed."

"Tyler went alone?" Clay asked in surprise. "I thought Ricky Mercado was going to Central America with him."

"Ricky's there," Flynt assured him. "But we've all agreed that Ricky should stay at the military base with Luke while Tyler meets with the Spanish interpreter.

In case Tyler encounters any trouble along the way,'' he explained further.

Clay nodded. ''Probably wise. If they stayed together…'' He let the comment hang unfinished, but he knew by Flynt's frown that he understood the warning. If the men remained together and were captured by the terrorists, the rescue mission would fail.

''Yeah,'' Flynt agreed. ''That's what we thought, too.'' He forced a smile, though Clay knew it was for his benefit. Flynt's concern for his friends wouldn't end until his buddies returned to the States with Westin in tow.

Flynt reared back in his chair. ''So what brings you to the offices of the Lone Star Country Club? Don't tell me Fiona has talked you into applying for membership.''

Reminded of his purpose for dropping by to see Flynt, Clay blew out a breath. ''No. I wanted to talk to you about Fiona.'' He related the events of the afternoon, from Fiona's driving off without paying for her gas to her arrest.

When he finished, Flynt shook his head wearily. ''Looks as if she's up to her old tricks.''

Frowning, Clay leaned forward, bracing his elbows on his knees. ''Why does she continue to pull these stunts? I would've thought she'd outgrown these kinds of pranks years ago.''

''Yeah,'' Flynt agreed, ''most people would have. But you'd have to know Fiona's childhood to understand what feeds her need for attention.''

Clay sank back in his chair. "Enlighten me."

"It all goes back to when she and Cara were born," Flynt began. "They're identical twins. Mirror twins," he clarified.

"Yeah. So?"

"There was a problem during the birth. Nothing life-threatening," he added quickly at Clay's startled look. "But Cara had some complications. Had to do with her breathing. Fiona was born first and without a problem, but Cara's delivery was slower." He lifted a shoulder. "I can't begin to explain all the medical mumbo jumbo, but the gist of it is, Cara required more medical attention. Mother was allowed to take Fiona home, but Cara had to spend several weeks in the neonatal unit at the hospital. Even after she was allowed to come home, her vitals had to be monitored around the clock." He shuddered, remembering. "Scared the hell out of my folks. All of us, for that matter, though I was really too young to fully understand what was going on. Fiona was healthy, strong. Cara was weaker and needed more care." Flynt lifted his hands. "I think you can see the problem."

"You're telling me that Fiona's behavior stems from Cara getting more attention when they were babies?" He shook his head. "Sorry. I don't buy that."

Flynt braced his arms on the desk and leaned forward, his gaze intense. "But it didn't stop when they were babies. Not that my parents favored one over the other," he said in his parents' defense. "But everyone was more careful with Cara. She was quieter than Fiona, less energetic, definitely less outgoing. Cara had only to sneeze and everyone was all over her, fussing over her, taking her temperature. You get the picture.''

Clay nodded grimly. "Yeah. I'm afraid I do. Fiona wanted your parents' attention and discovered that she could get it by acting out.''

Flynt nodded. "Exactly. The crazier and more bizarre the behavior, the more attention she received. It didn't seem to matter to her that the attention was negative. It was attention, and attention was what she wanted.''

Clay frowned. "It's hard to believe that a twenty-seven-year-old woman wouldn't have figured that out by now.''

Flynt lifted a brow, and Clay snorted a laugh. "Sorry. I forgot for a moment that we were talking about Fiona.''

Clay lay on his back in his bed, his hands folded behind his head, staring at the dark ceiling. Though he was exhausted, sleep wouldn't come. The conversation he'd had with Flynt kept running over and over again through his mind. Though he didn't approve of Fiona's behavior, he was beginning to understand what motivated her. Amazingly he even felt a little bit sorry for her.

A soft tap sounded at his door. Startled, he lifted his head. "Yeah?''

The door opened a crack. "Clay? May I come in?"

He yanked the sheet over his legs and sat up, tucking it around his waist. "Yeah. Sure."

The door opened wider and Fiona stepped inside. Unable to see her in the darkness, he reached over to switch on the bedside lamp, praying she wasn't wearing the same getup she'd had on that morning. When he turned back, she stood at the foot of his bed, her hands clutched nervously at her waist. Good. She was still dressed in the same outfit she'd had on that afternoon at the police station.

"Is something wrong?"

She shook her head. "No. I...I just wanted to say I was sorry."

If she'd announced she was pregnant, she couldn't have surprised him more. He eyed her suspiciously, wondering if this wasn't another ploy of hers to drive him crazy.

But then he saw the sheen of tears in her eyes, and he realized this was no game.

"Forget it," he said. "It's over."

"You don't hate me?"

He snorted a laugh and shook his head. "No, I don't hate you."

Her shoulders sagged in relief. He thought she'd leave then, but she gripped her hands more tightly together and took a step closer to the bed. "Clay?"

"Yeah?"

She opened her mouth as if she was about to say something, then closed it.

"Never mind." She turned to leave, but stopped in the doorway and looked back over her shoulder. "Clay?"

"Yeah?"

"I don't hate you, either."

Before he could respond, she stepped quickly out into the hall and closed the door behind her.

Ford accepted the glass of sparkling water from his wife and tried his best to hide his disappointment that it wasn't the martini he'd requested. "Thank you, dear."

Settling on the glider next to him, Grace placed a hand on his thigh and joined her gaze with his to look out over their land. "Oh, but it's good to be home," she said with a contented sigh.

Smiling, he wrapped an arm around her shoulders and drew her against his side. Although he'd enjoyed the freedom to smoke and drink whenever he pleased while she was away, that pleasure had lasted less than a day. "It's good to have you back. I missed you."

She looked up at him, her eyes softening as she met the warmth in his. "I missed you, too."

He leaned over to kiss her, then shifted, snuggling her more comfortably at his side, and turned his gaze back to the sunset.

"Anything exciting happen while I was away?" she asked after a moment.

He tensed at the innocently asked question. He'd

put off telling her about Fiona's arranged marriage for as long as he could, fearing she'd be angry with him.

Forcing the tension from his shoulders, he said, "As a matter of fact, something did."

She turned to peer at him. "Not another murder, I hope."

He shook his head. "No, nothing like that." Frowning, he drew his arm from around her. "There's no easy way to tell you this, Grace, so I might as well just spit it out and be done with it."

"What?" she asked, her forehead creasing in concern. "Ford, you're frightening me."

He took a deep breath, then said in a rush, "Fiona ran off and got married."

Her eyes shot wide. "Fiona? To whom?"

"Clay Martin."

"Clay Martin," she repeated incredulously, then laughed. "You old scoundrel," she scolded, and punched him playfully on the arm. "You shouldn't tease me that way. You nearly gave me a heart attack."

"This is no joke, Grace," he said, his expression grave. "But you haven't heard the worst of it yet."

She stared at him, her smile fading. "Oh, Ford," she murmured. "What have you done?"

Pursing his lips, he averted his gaze. "It was for her own good," he said defensively. "Clay's a good man. Honest. Hardworking. And tough enough to handle a fireball like our Fiona." He turned to frown at Grace. "You know how she is. Flitting from one relationship to another. Spending money like water. The girl is totally irresponsible and wouldn't know commitment if it knocked her upside the head.''

"Yes," Grace agreed. "But do you really think marriage is the answer?"

He shook his head and looked away again, staring at the slowly fading sunset, for the first time questioning his part in arranging the marriage. "I hope to God it is. Clay's a good man," he said again as if to convince himself. "He'll make Fiona a fine husband, if she'll let him."

"Yes," Grace said thoughtfully. "I've always liked Clay." She looked at Ford suspiciously. "But Fiona didn't go along with this willingly. I know my daughter better than to believe she would marry a man just because her father told her to."

"No," he admitted, feeling a stab of guilt. "It took some conniving. I approached Clay with the idea first and agreed to pay him a hundred thousand dollars if he'd marry Fiona and teach her the meaning of responsibility and commitment. Then I told Fiona that I'd arranged the marriage for her."

"And she went along without a fight?" she asked, her voice heavy with doubt.

He shook his head. "No. She kicked up a pretty big fuss, but I told her she didn't have a choice. Told her I was cutting her off. Closing all her bank and credit-card accounts."

"And did you?" she asked.

He nodded. "Damn right, I did. She'd never have gone along with the marriage otherwise."

They sat a moment in silence before Ford found the courage to look at his wife again. "Well?" he prodded. "Do you think I was wrong to interfere?"

Grace sighed. "Wrong or not, what's done is done." Then she smiled and tucked her arm through his. "But you were right about one thing," she said, resting her head against his shoulder. "If anyone can handle our Fiona, it's Clay Martin."

The next morning Fiona wandered out to the barn, still reeling from the phone conversation she'd just had with her mother. To her amazement—and utter disappointment—her mother had called to offer her congratulations on her and Clay's marriage.

Clay glanced up from the engine he was working on as Fiona stepped into the barn. When he saw her expression, he straightened in alarm. "What's wrong?"

She shrugged. "I just talked to Mom."

"She's back from her visit with Cara in the Middle East?"

Fiona nodded and climbed onto a sawhorse to sit. "Her flight arrived late yesterday afternoon."

"Cara's okay, isn't she?"

Fiona dropped her elbows to her knees and her chin onto her fists. "Yes. According to Mom, she's absolutely glowing."

"Then why the long face?"

"Daddy told Mom about our elopement."

Clay picked up a rag and slowly wiped the grease from his hands, watching her carefully. "Is she mad?"

She shook her head. "No. In fact, she couldn't be happier."

"That's good, isn't it?"

She dropped down from the sawhorse. "No, it's not good!" she cried. "I was sure Mom would be furious with Daddy for arranging this stupid marriage and she'd make him get it annulled."

"And she's not?"

"Are you kidding? She's already planning a reception in our honor!"

"A reception?"

"Yes. A big one. And if I know my mother, which I do, she'll invite half the town."

"A reception," he repeated, beginning to feel a little sick himself.

"Yes, and we'll be on display for all the town to gawk at. The happily married couple," she said bitterly. "What a joke."

"Do we have to go?"

Fiona slowly lifted her head. "We don't if we're not married."

"But we *are* married," he said in frustration. "That's the problem."

"Yeah, but we don't have to stay married." She paced, anxious to make him see things her way. "You don't want to be married to me any more than I want to be married to you, so why not end the charade?"

He scowled at her. "We can't. Remember? Your father and I made a deal. It's just for two months. Besides," he said, waving away her suggestion, "he'll cut you off without a cent if we end the marriage."

"But Daddy only wanted us to marry because he was worried that I wouldn't be able to take care of myself if something were to happen to him. If you were to convince him that I *am* capable of taking care of myself, he'd let us get an annulment. I just know he would."

Clay listened, tempted. She made it sound so easy. The two-month stipulation he'd agreed to didn't matter, not if Carson was getting what he'd wanted from Clay. Granted, everything Clay would tell Carson about Fiona would be a lie, but Clay was living a lie as it was, so what difference would it make if he told another to void the first?

As far as the money went, her father had already deposited the entire amount into Clay's account, so Carson would have to sue Clay to get it back, and the burden of proof would be on Carson's back, not Clay's. And if Carson did sue, the case would probably be tied up in court for years, which would give Clay plenty of time to turn the ranch into a profitable business and save the money he needed to pay Carson back the original hundred thousand, plus interest.

He shook his head, unable to believe he was even considering this. "No," he said, turning his back to her. "I won't do it."

Fiona stomped her foot. "Why not?" she cried.

"You don't want to be stuck in this miserable marriage any more than I do."

He glanced over his shoulder and lifted a brow. "Who says I don't?"

Armed with tweezers, Fiona leaned as close to the bathroom mirror as she could without climbing into the sink while searching her eyebrows for any strays that needed to be plucked. Finding one, she fitted the tweezers over it, squeezed her eyes shut and gave a yank.

Yelping, she dropped the tweezers and hopped up and down, holding her hand to her brow until the stinging subsided. When it had, she squared her shoulders and approached the mirror again, muttering under her breath, "I'd give my right arm for the money to have my eyebrows professionally waxed."

"Fiona?"

At the sound of Clay's voice coming from the other side of the closed door, she added under her breath, "Make that *his* right arm," then called in a louder voice, "What?"

"Are you okay?"

She inspected her brow, frowning. "I'm fine."

"I thought I heard you yell. Sounded like you were in pain or something. What are you doing in there?"

She sighed in frustration, then turned and twisted open the door. "Going crazy," she snapped, then pushed past him. Snatching a brush from her bedside table, she bent at the waist, dropping her head to let hair fall around her face. She dragged the brush from her nape to the ends of her hair in fast, jerky strokes.

Clay watched, a frown creasing his forehead. "Are you mad about something?"

She snapped upright, her dark hair flying back to fall behind her shoulders. "Mad?" she repeated, her eyes wild. "I'm bored out of my mind!"

Though he was sure she wouldn't appreciate the humor, Clay couldn't help but laugh.

She wagged the brush at him. "Don't you dare laugh at me, Clay Martin. This isn't funny."

He held up a hand, trying his best to hide his smile. "I'm sure it's not. So why don't you do something if you're bored?"

"Like what? I'm broke, remember? This week's allowance went to pay my fines."

"There are things you can do that don't cost money."

"Oh, really," she said dryly. "And what would you suggest I do?"

"You could watch television."

Scowling, she turned away, tossing the brush to the bed. "I'm sick of watching television."

"You could cook."

"I don't know how."

"Read?"

"Puts me to sleep."

"I guess that rules out taking a nap." He hesitated a moment, sure he would regret the offer, then decided, what the hell. She probably wouldn't accept, anyway. "I'm going outside to work on the fence. You could come along and help if you want."

She sent him a withering look. "Tempting, but I think I'll pass."

He shrugged and turned for the door. "Suit yourself."

Fiona listened to the sound of his footsteps fading, then the slam of the back door. Panicked at the thought of spending another afternoon in the house with no one but herself for company, she ran after him. "Clay, wait!"

Seven

Fiona sat in the shade of the truck, her back pressed against the rear tire, her legs stretched out in front of her, lazily fanning herself with her wide-brimmed straw hat while she watched Clay work. Though she'd never admit it, she found watching him string barbed wire much more interesting than anything daytime television had to offer. Not that the conversation was particularly stimulating, she reminded herself. He hadn't said more than two words to her in the hour they'd been outside. But she certainly couldn't fault the view. And since he was absorbed in his task, she was free to look all she wanted.

He'd dressed for the work at hand and had traded the khaki slacks and white, starched shirt he wore while on duty for a faded chambray shirt, worn jeans and scuffed boots. In deference to the heat of the midday sun, he'd rolled the cuffs of the long-sleeve shirt to his elbows, exposing dark, hairy forearms that glistened with perspiration. Stained leather work gloves covered his wide hands to his wrists, protecting his palms and fingers from the wire's sharp barbs. A leather belt cinched his jeans at his waist. Another wider belt holding an assortment of tools rode low on his hips. Beneath it all lay rippling muscle.

With years of experience to back her claim, Fiona considered herself a connoisseur of the male anatomy. Clay Martin definitely met her high standards for the perfectly formed man.

He bent to unroll another length of wire from the spool and his shirt stretched taut across his back. The fabric clung to his skin, damp with perspiration. She didn't know how he stood it.

"Wouldn't you be cooler if you took off your shirt?"

He pulled a staple from between his teeth and drove it into the post, securing the wire. "Probably."

"Then why don't you?"

He straightened and shoved back his hat to wipe the sweat from his brow. "Skin cancer."

"You have skin cancer?" she asked in alarm.

"No. And I don't intend to get it, either."

She frowned at his back as he strode to the next post, then called after him, "You can die from heat stroke the same as you can from skin cancer."

"Bring me another handful of those staples."

Huffing out a breath at his stubbornness, she dug a handful of staples from the sack and pushed to her feet. "Mule-headed man," she muttered, then thrust her hand at him. "Here're your staples. I hope you choke on them."

Grinning at her, he plucked a few from her palm

and popped them into his mouth. "And who would look after you if I choked to death?" he teased.

"Me," she said emphatically.

He laughed as he fitted one of the staples over the wire. "How? Last I heard, bitching wasn't a career."

She dropped her jaw. "Bitching!" she repeated. "Is that all you think I'm capable of doing?"

He pulled another staple from his mouth and hunkered down, centering it over the wire. "That's all I've seen or heard you do."

"I'll have you know I can do a lot of things," she said indignantly.

He turned on the balls of his feet to look up at her. "Name one."

"I can..." She stopped and frowned, unable to think of a single skill to offer in her defense.

He turned back around and lifted the hammer to drive in the staple. "That's what I thought."

Fiona grabbed the tool and wrenched it from his hand. "I may not have a lengthy résumé of marketable skills, but I can swing a hammer as well as you any day of the week."

He held up a staple. "Prove it."

Jutting her chin, she snatched the staple from his hand, then pushed past him and positioned it over the wire. Catching her lip between her teeth, she raised the hammer and brought it down, putting all her strength in the effort.

Smug, she stepped back and gestured toward the post. "See? I told you I could do it."

He held up another staple. "Beginner's luck."

Accepting the challenge, she drove in a second. This time it took two swings to bury the staple. By the time she finished, perspiration beaded her brow.

He held up a third.

Scowling, she snatched it from his hand. She missed on the first swing, then firmed her lips and took two more, sinking it on the third.

"Wouldn't you be cooler if you took off your shirt?"

She shot him a look that let him know what he could do with his suggestion.

He lifted a shoulder. "What's good for the goose…"

In spite of her frustration with him, Fiona found herself laughing. She touched the head of the hammer to her temple in a salute. "Touché."

He stood and took the hammer from her hand. "Thanks. You just proved the point I was trying to make earlier."

"And what was that?"

He slipped the hammer into a loop on his tool belt, then slung a companionable arm around her shoulders and headed her for the next post. "That there are things you can do that don't cost money." He bumped his hip against hers, laughing when she stumbled sideways, off balance. "And have a little fun while you're at it," he added.

He ducked, laughing, when she took a swing at his head.

* * *

Groaning, Fiona crawled into bed and rolled to her side, pulling the covers over her head. She couldn't remember being this tired in her entire life. She ached in places she didn't know could ache. Her arms, her legs, her back, her hands. Even her butt muscles hurt from all the stooping and squatting required to pound all those stupid staples in place.

But she'd done it, she thought proudly. She'd matched Clay swing for swing, working alongside him throughout the rest of the day. And she'd done it without bitching even once. Well, maybe once, she amended reluctantly, remembering when she'd missed the staple and hit her thumb with the hammer. But that was understandable. Clay had grumbled a few times himself when barbs had pierced his gloves and pricked his skin.

The biggest surprise of all, though, was that she'd had fun. Imagine that, she thought, marveling at the oddity. Fiona Carson actually enjoying manual labor. If her father knew how she'd spent the afternoon, he'd probably have another heart attack.

Her amusement faded at the thought.

She couldn't imagine her life without her father in it. She loved him. Adored him. In spite of the fact that he'd forced her into this ridiculous marriage. Though she didn't agree with his methods, she knew he'd only done what he'd thought best for her. But if something should happen to him, as he feared, and she was left on her own, she knew she could take care of herself.

She didn't need Clay Martin or any other man looking after her.

Her thoughts segued to Clay. She frowned, trying to remember something he'd said to her the week before. They'd been talking about the reception her mother was planning in their honor, and Fiona had suggested that they end the charade, claiming that he didn't want to be stuck in this miserable marriage any more than she did.

Who says I don't?

She stiffened as his words pushed into her mind. Did he want to be married to her? she wondered. At the time he'd posed the question, she'd been upset and hadn't really paid attention to his reply. Now she wondered…

She tried to rebuild the scene in her mind, capturing his exact expression and mood at that precise moment. He'd been working in the barn when she'd sought him out, but had stopped his work when she'd told him about the reception. She distinctly remembered his expression then. His face had gone slack and the color had drained from his skin. He'd looked as if the idea of attending a reception in their honor sickened him as much as it did her.

But what about when he'd made the reply? she asked herself. What was his expression then? She squeezed her fingers against her temples, trying to remember. He'd had his back to her when she'd made the comment about him wanting out of the marriage as much as she did. He'd looked over his shoulder at her then, raised a brow in challenge and said, ''Who says I don't?''

Had he been serious? Or was he just being his normal contrary self? As hard as she puzzled over both his words and his expression, she couldn't decide.

With a sigh of defeat, she nestled her cheek deeper into the pillow and closed her eyes.

As her mind grew fuzzy with sleep, vignettes of her time with Clay drifted behind her closed lids. Clay standing with his boot propped on Roger's chest the night he'd caught them skinny-dipping, looking all macho and tough. Clay standing as stiff as a soldier beside her while they'd repeated their vows, his hand gripped tightly around her elbow. Clay hunkered down on the ground, looking up at her, a brow arched in challenge, as he offered a staple to her. Clay walking with his arm slung around her shoulders, his stride long, bumping his hip playfully against hers.

Being married to Clay wasn't so bad, she told herself. Things could be a lot worse.

Her daddy could have arranged for her to marry Roger Billings.

The door to the interrogation room opened and a young dispatcher stuck her head inside. ''Sorry to interrupt, Ranger Martin, but your wife's on line one. She said it was an emergency.''

Clay bit back his irritation at the interruption. ''Probably broke a fingernail,'' he muttered under his breath. He shoved the legal pad he'd scribbled his notes on in front of the officer sitting next to him. "I'll be right back."

He strode from the room and snatched a phone from the first desk he passed. "What?" he snapped into the receiver.

"Clay, where are you? You were supposed to be home more than an hour ago."

He groaned, having completely forgotten about the reception. "What time is it?"

"Almost six, and the party starts at seven."

He glanced over his shoulder at the closed door to the interrogation room. "Listen, Fiona. Something's come up."

"What? But, Clay, we're the guests of honor, for God's sake! We *have* to be there."

He rubbed at the headache that throbbed to life between his eyes. "Fiona, I'm in the middle of an interrogation," he said, struggling for patience. "I can't leave now. Go on without me. I'll meet you there as soon as I can."

"Oh, my God! I can't! What will people think if I arrive alone?"

Her hysterics broke the last thin hold he had on his patience. He closed his fingers in a chokehold on the receiver. "Listen and listen good," he said through clenched teeth. "That slimeball in the other room is a three-time sex offender who's walked every damn time because we never had enough evidence to nail him. I'm not leaving here to attend some damn party until I've sweated a full confession out of him. Understand?''

Before she could reply, he slammed the phone down in her ear.

By the time Clay had his confession, drove home and changed clothes, then made the long drive back to town to the country club, the party was in full swing.

Fiona hadn't exaggerated, he thought as he stood in the doorway, searching for her in the crowd of people who filled the Empire Room. If anything, her claim that her mother would invite half the town had been on the conservative side. Guests filled every inch of the expansive room and spilled out onto the adjoining gardens through the open French doors.

The elaborately set dining tables normally found in the restaurant were gone, replaced with smaller linen-topped round tables strategically arranged around the room's outer edges to create a dance floor in its center. Between the twin sets of French doors that opened to the garden, heavily laden buffet tables formed an elongated T. In the cross of the T, a silver punch bowl the size of a small lake served as a roost of sorts for two lovebirds carved from ice. Champagne spilled in a never-ending waterfall from around the sculpture's base and into the silver bowl.

Carrying his gaze farther, Clay caught a glimpse of Fiona surrounded by a large group of male admirers to the left of the buffet table. He hesitated a moment longer, trying to gauge her mood. He knew he'd been a little rough with her on the phone. No, he amended, he'd been downright ruthless. But she'd pushed him to the end of his rope with her hysterics about what people would think if she showed up alone. To Clay, it was just one more indication of her selfishness.

As he continued to stare at her, one of the men in the circle turned away, exposing her fully. The sight of her was like taking a bullet in the chest. Dressed in an ankle-length column of shimmering white, she looked like an angel, a queen… Hell, he thought, she looked like a bride.

Bits of baby's breath peeked from the loose curls she'd piled on top of her head, and a band of tiny seed pearls circled the smooth column of her neck. She wore no other adornments. But she didn't need any. Her beauty alone created more dazzle than a million precious stones.

He'd expected to find her storming around, cursing his very existence. Instead, she appeared to be enjoying the attention showered on her. But as he started toward her, he had to reconsider that first assessment. He detected a strain in her smile, a slight tremble in the fingers she curled around a glass of champagne, a sheen to her eyes that looked as if she were dangerously close to tears.

She was scared, he realized with a start. Terrified that he wasn't going to show up and she would be humiliated in front of the entire town.

He ought to turn right around and leave, he told

himself. Let her suffer whatever social disgrace his absence might cause her. Maybe that would knock her off her high horse, drain a little air out of that inflated ego of hers.

But then he caught a glimpse of the plastic bandage wrapped around her thumb and saw her again as she'd looked the day before, squared off before that post, her lip caught between her teeth in determination as she prepared for the first swing. She'd probably never held a hammer in her life, but that hadn't stopped her from accepting his challenge. If she'd accomplished nothing else that day, she'd proved to him she was no prima donna. She was spirited. Gutsy. Determined.

And, at the moment, scared to death.

He couldn't walk away, he told himself. Not when she looked so frightened, not when she looked so much like a bride.

Carson had paid him to do a job, he reminded himself. And though playing the role of the loving groom had never been part of their agreement, by God, he'd play the part tonight.

"There he is!" he heard someone shout. "The groom finally decided to show up!"

Fiona snapped up her head at the announcement, and their eyes met across the crowded room.

"Clay," she murmured, going all but limp with relief as he reached her. "You came."

He didn't bother to respond, but took the champagne glass from her hand and curved an arm around her waist. With everyone in the room now watching, he bent his head over hers, bowing her back, and kissed her with a passion that had every blue-haired woman in the room clucking her tongue—and every young one sighing with envy.

As he slowly straightened to meet her gaze, he dragged a hand down her arm and laced his fingers with her. "Sorry I'm late," he said, surprised to find his voice husky.

She stared up at him as if dazed. "I...it doesn't matter."

He bent to touch his mouth to hers again, this kiss briefer than the one before, yet degrees more intimate. "You look beautiful," he said, and gave her hand a squeeze.

She gulped, staring. "Thank you."

He shifted, keeping an arm around her waist, and turned to face the guests that had gathered around. He lifted the glass of champagne.

"I'd like to make a toast," he said, raising his voice to reach the far corners of the room. He waited until the music had stopped and the guests had quieted. "To the most beautiful woman in the world," he said, then looked down at Fiona. "My wife, Fiona Carson Martin."

He watched her eyes fill and knew that he'd chosen just the right words, just the right way in which to put her fears of social disgrace to rest. He took a sip of the champagne, then held it to her lips for her to drink.

As he did, the orchestra struck up again. Clay recognized the song as one Nat King Cole had made fa-

mous. "Unforgettable." That was exactly what he
planned to make this night for Fiona.

He passed the glass to the man standing next to him.
"Would you mind holding this for me? I think they're
playing our song."

With his gaze on Fiona's, he drew her arm through
the bend of his. The crowd parted, creating a pathway
for them as he escorted her to the dance floor. Holding
her hand above her head, he spun her in a dizzying
pirouette, then swept her into his arms.

Breathless, she cupped her fingers at his neck, then
laid her cheek against his. "Thank you," she whispered.

He heard the tremble in her voice, the gratitude, and
swooped her low in a heart-stopping dip over his knee.
"Just part of the job, ma'am," he replied with a wink.

But as the night wore on, Clay began to feel less
and less as if this was a job. And he didn't feel so
much like an actor in a well-staged play, either. Standing with his arm draped around Fiona's shoulders or
twining his fingers through hers or stealing a kiss felt
natural somehow. Right.

And by the time he cut a slice of the towering wedding cake her mother had custom-ordered and flown
from an exclusive bakery in New York and fed a piece
of it to Fiona, he was sure he felt every emotion a real
groom must feel at that moment. Happy. Giddy. Ex-
pectant. Laughing as he'd watched her lick from her
lips the globs of icing he'd purposely smeared there.

Feeling the slow spill of desire through his groin when their gazes met over matching silver goblets, their arms linked in a symbol of unity, as they'd toasted their future together with champagne.

And later, when the lights had dimmed and they'd danced again beneath a canopy of stars in the garden, their bodies swaying sensually, he'd experienced a contentment that had permeated his entire body, wrapped itself around his heart.

For a moment, the length of one magical evening really, Clay felt like a man in love and Fiona his adoring bride.

As was expected as the guests of honor, Fiona and Clay were the last guests to leave the party.

Fiona's mother called to them just as they reached the door. "Just a minute, you two!"

They turned in unison and waited while she hurried toward them.

"I haven't had a chance to say two words to you all evening," she complained good-naturedly. She smiled and lifted her hands to frame her daughter's face between her palms. "My baby," she murmured, tears filling her eyes. She pressed a kiss to Fiona's cheek, then caught her hand and squeezed. "I'm so happy for you, darling. So very, very happy." She turned to smile at Clay, including him in her good wishes. "For both of you."

She reached to clasp Clay's hand. "I've always liked you, Clay," she said, and gave his hand an affectionate squeeze. "And I want you to know that I'm honored to have you as my son-in-law."

Clay wasn't sure what to say. The woman was acting as if this was a real marriage. Hadn't Carson told his wife the details of their arrangement? "Thank you, Mrs. Carson," was the only reply he could think to offer.

"Mrs. Carson," she repeated, clucking her tongue. "We'll have none of that. You'll call me Mother the same as my other children." She laughed. "You may not realize it yet, but when you marry into the Carson clan, you get the whole dang family, warts and all."

Clay stared, stunned by her warmth, her sincerity.

She gave their hands one last squeeze, then released them. "I'm sure you're both exhausted and anxious to be on your way, but I have a little surprise for you." She pulled a white silk ribbon from beneath the gauzy folds of the collar of her blouse and lifted it over her head. A gold key dangled at its end.

She smiled and pressed the key into Clay's hand. "I know you two haven't had a chance to take a proper honeymoon yet, so I thought you might enjoy a weekend in the country club fantasy suite as a gift from Ford and me."

Clay stole a look at Fiona, but she was already reaching to give her mother a tearful hug.

Grace drew back, sniffing, then pushed her hands at the two of them, shooing them away. "Go on now," she ordered, "and don't worry about a thing. I've had the suite completely outfitted with everything you will need."

Clay slid the key into the lock, then twisted the knob and pushed open the door. The sound of soft piano music and the fragrance of roses drifted out to greet them.

He didn't dare look at Fiona. If he did, he was afraid he'd get sucked right back into the bride-and-groom fantasy that had woven itself around him during the reception. When she didn't make a move to enter, he placed a hand low on her back to nudge her into the room. She balked.

He looked down at her. "What?" he said in frustration.

"You're supposed to carry me over the threshold," she whispered, and tipped her head discreetly in the direction they'd come.

He glanced to his left and saw a couple in the hallway, poised before another door, watching and waiting expectantly.

Muttering a curse under his breath, he stooped, caught her beneath the knees and swept her up into his arms.

She looped an arm around his shoulders, fluttered two fingers at the couple, then rested her head on his shoulder with a dramatic sigh.

The feel of her in his arms was almost too much. He bolted across the threshold, kicked the door closed behind them and plopped her down on her feet.

"Oh, look!" she cried, and rushed across the room to bury her nose in a cloud of white roses that filled the cut-crystal vase perched on a linen-draped table in front of the French doors. Lifting her head with a sigh, she moved to look down at the gardens and fountain below. "Isn't the view gorgeous?" she said dreamily, hugging herself.

Clay stood rooted to the spot, wishing he was anywhere but here. If he lasted ten minutes without consummating this marriage, he'd consider himself lucky. He shrugged off his jacket and tossed it over a chair. "It's all right."

She glanced over her shoulder at him. "Well, don't get too carried away."

Scowling, he tugged at the knot of his tie, loosening it. "Couldn't we just go home? Your mother would never know the difference."

"She'd hear about it before we made it to the front gate," she informed him. "Staff talk."

He groaned and ripped the tie over his head, knowing she was right.

She lifted her hands. "Why not just relax and enjoy yourself? That's what I plan to do." She turned and pulled a bottle of champagne from a silver ice bucket. With a nod of approval at the vintage, she plunged the bottle back into the ice and moved on around the table.

"Mother even ordered caviar," she said, laughing with delight at the discovery. She scraped a cracker over the glistening black mound and popped it into her mouth, then glanced back at Clay. "Want some?"

He stuck his hands in his pockets and shook his head. "No thanks."

She lifted a shoulder, then left the table to explore the rest of the room. She opened a door and peeked inside. With a squeal, she darted through the opening and disappeared from sight. "Oh, my God, Clay!" she cried. "Come quick! You've got to see this."

He closed his eyes, offered up a prayer for self-control, then crossed to the doorway. "Fiona..." he began, hoping there was still a chance he could convince her to leave.

The words dried up in his mouth at the sight that greeted him. She lay in the middle of a huge round bed, propped against a mountain of white pillows, her hands folded behind her head, her feet bare, her legs crossed at the ankles.

He tore his gaze away to look around the room. Candlelight flickered from every surface, while shimmering gold fabric draped the ceiling and walls, giving the room the illusion of a tent spun from gold.

"Isn't this terrific?" she exclaimed. "It's like something from *Arabian Nights*."

Before he could answer, she waved a hand at his feet. "Take off your boots."

Without questioning why, he tugged off his boots and socks and tossed them aside. He bit back a groan as his feet sank into the plush carpet.

"Doesn't it feel as if you're walking on air?" Smiling, she stretched out on her stomach, pushing her legs out behind her, and splayed her hands over the thick, white fur that covered the bed. She moaned, burying her face in the luxurious pelt. "This is positively decadent."

She lifted a hand, gesturing blindly for him to join her. "You've got to try this," she said, her voice muffled by the spread, then rolled to her back and closed her eyes with a sigh. "It's like floating on a cloud."

When he didn't respond, she craned her neck to look behind her and held out a hand. "Come on," she urged.

Though he was sure he'd regret it later, Clay found himself crossing the room and placing his hand in hers. She looked up at him and smiled. At that moment he knew he never stood a chance.

Upon reflection, he could see that the whole evening had built to this moment, weaving him in a fantasy of brides and grooms and weddings. He felt like a groom on his wedding night, had the needs of a groom. And before him lay his bride. He dropped onto a knee on the mattress and lay down beside her.

"Wait," she said.

She scooted to the opposite side of the bed, retrieved something from the end table, then lay back down beside him, a controller gripped in her hand. "Watch this," she whispered, and pointed the device at the ceiling.

Though he would have preferred to look at her, Clay shifted his gaze and watched the ceiling part, gliding silently back on hidden tracks and revealing a blue-black sky filled with twinkling stars.

"I'd heard about this," she murmured, her voice soft with wonder, "but I've never seen it before."

Clay felt a slight movement, then the slow, silken slide of her fingers linking with his. He turned his head to peer at her and emotion filled his throat. "Fiona?"

She pressed another button and the mournful wail of a sax spilled from speakers hidden somewhere in the room, blending with the heady scent of roses and molten wax that already filled the air. She pushed yet another, and the bed began to slowly turn. Clay had felt off balance before. Now he felt as if he were free-falling, without a parachute to break his fall.

"Fiona," he said again, her name a hoarse whisper that scraped along his raw throat.

She turned her head to the side, her lips curving in a slow smile as she met his gaze. "It's magic," she whispered. "You feel it, too, don't you?"

Lifting himself to an elbow, he plucked a pin from her hair, then brought his gaze back to hers. "The only thing I want to feel right now is you."

Eight

Her smile slowly melted as he found another pin, removed it and tossed it aside. Another, and her hair tumbled to her shoulders. He pushed his fingers through the tangle of curls, holding her face to his, and lowered his head. He touched his lips to hers once, retreated, then touched them again. He sipped slowly, tenderly, then, sensing her acceptance, opened his mouth over hers and drank deeply. Her flavor slid through him in waves, an intoxicating blend of tastes and textures that left him aching for more. He shifted higher, forcing her head back against the pillows, and deepened the kiss, giving, taking, wanting more. Always more.

He dragged his fingers from her hair, smoothed them down the side of her neck, her skin like satin, soft, sleek, warm beneath his callused hand. He shaped his fingers around her throat, felt the thrum of her pulse in the hollow that lay beneath his palm.

Her lips parted on a moan, and he swallowed the sound, then thrust his tongue into her mouth, probing, teasing, tasting. He found her tongue, mated it with his, then plunged deeper. He felt her arch beneath him and reveled in the feel of her body reaching hungrily for his.

Dragging his mouth from hers, he dipped his head lower. "More," he whispered, and opened his mouth over her breast. She gasped, fisting her fingers in his hair as he swept his tongue across her covered nipple.

Frustrated by the fabric that kept him from tasting her fully, he sat up, drawing her up, as well. He saw the wonder in her gaze, the passion. Humbled by it, he touched his hand to her cheek, the caress reverent, tender. Then slowly he let his hand drift down, his fingers skimming over her breasts, gliding over her abdomen, until they rested on the bunched fabric of her dress at her knee. He gathered the fabric in his fist, pushed it along her thigh. When she shivered, her eyes shuttering closed, he captured her mouth again, soothing her, teasing her, as he eased the dress from beneath her hips.

He broke the kiss only long enough to tug the dress over her head, then found her mouth with his again and filled his hands with her breasts. He groaned at the softness, the fullness that strained against his hands, the turgidity of the nipples that stabbed at his palms. Desperate to taste her there, as well, he pushed her back on the bed and shifted his body lower. He blew a breath across her breast, warming it, then stroked his tongue across her nipple. She groaned, holding his head to her.

"You like that?" he murmured, raking his tongue across her nipple again. He felt the scrape of her nails against his scalp, her shudder, and smiled. "Yeah. Me, too." He opened his mouth over her breast, then closed his lips around the rosy, sweet center and suckled, drawing her in.

She bucked wildly beneath him, his name rushing past her lips on a gust of air, a whimper, a plea. He felt her hands on his back, the impatient tug of her fingers as she tried to pull his shirt free from his slacks. As anxious as she to get rid of the barrier, he reached over his shoulder and dragged the shirt over his head. The sleeves snagged at his wrists, held by the buttons that secured the cuffs. He jerked, and the buttons popped free, flying across the room.

He dropped the shirt over the side of the bed and sank back over her. "Now," he said, with a sigh. He gathered her breasts between his hands and brought them together, feasting on first one nipple, then the other. He felt the shiver that rippled through her, and buried his face in the valley between. He inhaled deeply. "I love the way you smell," he murmured, then rooted deeper to sweep his tongue along the narrow valley. He shifted higher, dragging his body up hers to touch his lips to hers. "And the way you taste."

He felt the tremble in her arms as she wrapped them around him, the heat in each individual finger as she caressed the nape of his neck. Her touch was soothing, electrifying. It had been months since he'd experienced the pleasure of a woman's hands on his flesh. Perhaps never at the depth with which his body was responding to Fiona's. He felt a sudden, almost desperate need to wrap his arms around her and burrow deep inside, to soak up all the warmth and softness she had to offer, until their bodies and their hearts converged into one.

Her touch became greedy, setting nerve endings on fire as she swept her palms over his back. Her fingers stilled midway down, and he stiffened, remembering too late the ugly scars that traversed his spine. He felt the change in her immediately, tasted it. The hesitation. The curiosity. Knew the revulsion that would follow. Fisting his hands against the mattress, he heaved himself up, forcing her arms from around him and their mouths apart. He rolled from her and to his feet.

Though the lighting was dim—a circumstance he was now grateful for—he sensed the question in her eyes even before she found her voice.

But the word "what" was all she managed to get past her lips.

He snatched his shirt from the floor and shrugged it on, turning his back to her. "An old injury," he said gruffly.

He heard a rustle of movement behind him, felt her hand alight on his back, and he stiffened, his fingers freezing on the button he was frantically trying to close. He detected a tremble in her touch. A hesitation. Revulsion? he thought again.

"Clay?"

He stepped away, breaking the contact. "This was

a mistake, Fiona,'' he said, his voice taut with anger.
''I should never have let it go this far.''

''But, Clay—''

''I said it was a mistake!'' he shouted, then strode
for the sitting room and slammed the door between
them.

Hours later Fiona lay on the round bed, alone, the
covers pulled to her chin, her eyes wide and unblink-
ing. A chill lay beneath her skin and iced her heart.
She'd never been rejected by a man before. She'd rejected plenty, sure, but she'd never been on the re-
ceiving end, had never experienced the devastating humiliation of being the one scorned.

She caught her lip between her teeth, as she remembered the anger in Clay's voice before he'd slammed
the door between them. He'd been mad. Furious! But
why? What had she done? One minute they were
locked in an embrace that even now, as she thought
of it, made her pulse leap. The next he was pushing
away from her.

A mistake, he'd called it. But was the mistake hers?
If so, what was it? Kissing him? Wanting him as badly
as he'd seemed to want her?

She closed her eyes against the tears that burned.
And, oh, how she'd wanted him. She still did. Even
after he'd rejected her. She'd never tasted such passion
in a man, never had one make her want with the fer-
vency she had wanted Clay. She'd offered herself

freely to him, returned his passion with one she was sure rivaled his own.

And he'd left her, slamming the door between them, telling her it was a mistake.

But where was the mistake? she cried silently. She went back over her every move, reviewing her every word, mentally reenacting the scene from the moment he'd first kissed her until he'd pushed her away.

Her eyes shot open wide.

The scar, she remembered. Right after her fingers had bumped over the narrow channel of scar tissue on his back, he'd shoved her away. Was he self-conscious about the imperfection? she wondered, remembering how quickly he'd grabbed for his shirt and put it on. And, too, the day before, when he was working on the fence and she'd suggested he'd be cooler without his shirt, he'd refused to take it off. That was it, she told herself. It had to be. He was afraid she would find the scar a turnoff.

She threw back the covers and scooted from the bed. Well, she wasn't some frail little ninny who shrank in fear from something as trivial as a scar. A scar was nothing but a thickened layer of skin, a souvenir of sorts from an old injury. On some men, if not too severe, they even added character to an otherwise uninteresting face.

Determined to prove to Clay that his scar didn't bother her, she headed for the door. That she was naked didn't concern her. For what she had planned, clothing of any sort would only be a hindrance.

Twisting the knob slowly, she eased the door open a crack and peeked into the sitting room. He had pulled out the sofa bed to sleep on. She saw the shape of his body beneath the covers, his back to her, his face turned to the far wall. From the rhythmic sound of his breathing, she knew he slept. Which was in her favor, she told herself as she tiptoed across the room. If awake, he'd probably send her away before she had the opportunity to seduce him.

Lifting the edge of the covers, she slipped underneath, then scooted close to his back. After listening a moment to make sure he hadn't awakened, she placed her fingers at the nape of his neck and trailed them down his spine, until she found the scar. She was surprised to discover that it stretched from just beneath his left shoulder blade and ran in a jagged line to his waist. Emotion tightened her throat as she realized how much pain an injury of this magnitude must have caused him. With tears burning her eyes, she leaned to press her lips to the slender rope of flesh.

He stirred at her touch, and she jerked back, holding her breath until he stilled again. She waited a second longer, just to be sure he was asleep, then snuggled against his back and curved an arm over his waist.

Positioned as she was, she knew immediately that he was nude, which was, again, to her advantage. It also made her painfully aware of his buttocks. She'd noticed before how muscular his buttocks were, but there was a huge difference between observing his backside clothed and feeling it bared against her abdomen. Every nerve ending in her body seemed to have snapped to attention, their antennae tuned to the spot where their bodies met.

Easing her legs down the length of his, she was reminded how much longer his body was than hers, how much more muscled. And hairier, too, she thought as she drew her toes up the back of his leg. She pressed her face against his back, suppressing a giggle at the tickling sensation.

And his scent, she thought, her amusement fading as she became aware of it. She closed her eyes and inhaled deeply. Pure male with just a hint of soap lingering on his skin. Without conscious thought she ran her fingers over his chest and stomach, her touch light.

He shifted, pressing his buttocks more firmly into the bend of her body. After a moment he laced his fingers through hers, and settled again with a sigh, holding her hand against his chest.

She lay still as death, her eyes wide, her heart pounding like a symphony of bass drums. Heat spread slowly through her womb and out to every extremity. She was aroused. With one single move of his hips he'd shot her back into her earlier state of arousal. But, more, he'd touched the deepest region of her heart by drawing her hand to his chest and holding it there. She could feel the soft thump of his heartbeat against her palm, marveled at its steady rhythm, all but melted at the comforting warmth that seeped into her hand.

When she was sure she could draw a breath without sobbing, she pressed a trembling kiss to the center of his spine. She barely had time to move before he was rolling over and gathering her into his arms. Murmuring words she couldn't understand, he found her mouth, then closed his lips over hers with a shuddery sigh. His kiss turned passionate, painfully so, and bespoke a familiarity between them, an ease she knew only too well didn't exist. But she responded in kind, opening her heart and offering him all the emotions that welled up inside.

Was he awake? she wondered even as she wrapped her arms around his neck and drew his face closer. Or was he locked in some dream in which he thought she was someone else? She closed her eyes, refusing to consider the possibility, and held him more tightly. "Clay?"

That one word was all it took to break the spell.

A groan rose from deep in his chest, one filled with such pain, such need, she couldn't separate the two. Pulling away from her, he rolled her to her back and dropped his forehead to her chest. "No," he moaned. "This is wrong. A mistake."

"Please," she begged, stroking his hair with her hand. "I want this. You."

He lifted his head and she nearly wept at the despair she saw in his eyes.

"Please," she said again, bringing a hand to cradle his cheek.

She felt the tension that arced through him, drawing his body taut, sensed the urgency wound up inside him, watched the passion slowly burn the despair from his eyes. With his gaze on hers, he curled a hand around a breast and brought it to his mouth. His teeth scraped her nipple and she inhaled sharply, shocked by the sensations that rocked her. As the sensations settled low in her womb in an aching knot, she released her pent-up breath on a ragged sigh. Before she could draw another breath, he was lifting himself above her and forcing her legs apart with his knee.

Panicking, she said, "Clay, wait. I—"

Before she could explain, ask him to go slow, he thrust inside her, his hips slamming against hers. She gasped, digging her nails into his shoulders as pain ripped through her, leaving a trail of red-hot fire that exploded behind her tightly closed eyes.

His body turned to stone over hers.

She sensed his shock, understanding it.

"You're a virgin?"

She heard the disbelief in his voice and turned her face away, not wanting him to see her tears, her embarrassment. "Is that so hard to believe?"

He pushed back to look down at her. "Hell, yeah, it is. With your reputation, I would've thought you had slept with a dozen or more men by now."

She snapped her head around to glare at him. "For your information, I prized my virginity too much to give it away to just any man."

She saw the surprise flare in his eyes, the slow dawning as he realized what she'd inadvertently confessed. Furious with herself, she shoved angrily at his chest. "Get off me."

He caught her hands in his, gripping her fingers so tightly with his that her struggles to escape him were thwarted. "Why didn't you tell me?"

She looked away, too embarrassed to meet his gaze. "I—I tried."

He dropped his forehead to her chest. "Oh, God, Fiona." He groaned. "I'm sorry. I didn't realize. I swear. If I had…"

"What?" she demanded angrily. "How would your knowing I was a virgin have changed anything?"

He lifted his head to look at her, and she gulped at the regret, the guilt she found in his eyes.

"I would have been more gentle with you. I wouldn't have hurt you. I swear I would never have hurt you."

"But it's always painful the first time. I was prepared for that."

He tightened his fingers around hers. "It doesn't have to be." He shifted to lie beside her, still gripping her hand. "There are things a man can do to prepare a woman. To make it easier for her."

She sniffed, unsure whether to believe him. "What things?"

He inched closer and released her hand to splay his across her stomach. His fingers were wide and strong, but gentle as they kneaded her flesh.

"Things," he said again, his face now only inches from her own. He began to move his hand in slow, languid circles around her navel, each one larger than the one before. He brushed her lips with his. "Things like this," he whispered, and opened his hand over her mound.

She stiffened instinctively.

"Relax," he murmured. "I'm not going to hurt you."

She closed her eyes and forced herself to focus on his voice, allowing the soothing cadence of his words and the gentle pressure of his fingers to melt the tension from her body. He moved his hand lower, pushing two fingers along the narrow channel that led to her sex. She shivered, even as heat speared her center and turned it molten. She felt the pressure of his thumb against her opening and her legs jerked reflexively.

"Clay…"

She heard the panic in her voice and was shamed by it.

"Shh," he soothed, his lips a whispered caress on hers. "It's okay. It's just your body responding to my touch." He nuzzled her nose with his. "You're wet," he whispered as he circled his thumb in the moistness. "Can you feel the warmth?"

She nodded, afraid to open her mouth to reply for fear she'd beg. Even though she dreaded the pain, she wanted him inside her.

She caught his cheeks between her hands and brought his face to hers. She gulped at the passion in his eyes, the heat. "I think I'm ready," she said, her voice trembling.

He smiled, but shook his head. "Close. But not close enough."

He dropped to his back and drew her over him, arranging her knees on either side of his hips. With his gaze on hers, he shaped his hands over her breasts and gently squeezed. He chuckled when her eyes went wide. "Amazing, isn't it?" he said. "I touch you here—" he raked a thumb across her nipple, then dragged his hand down her stomach and slipped it between her legs "—and you feel it here."

She bucked as he molded his hand over her mound, her sex throbbing wildly beneath the exquisite pressure of his fingers. His smile softening, he curved a hand behind her neck and drew her down. She thought he intended to kiss her and gasped when, instead, at the last second, he dipped his head and caught her nipple between his teeth. Need twisted in her womb, a rope stretched to its limits, as he suckled, gently at first, then more greedily.

She clamped her knees at his hips, gasping. "Clay, please," she begged.

He rolled, turning her beneath him, and wedged his knee between her legs, spreading them apart. Holding himself above her, he smoothed a hand over her damp brow, his gaze on hers. "You're in control," he told her, and took her hand and guided it to his sex. "Nothing happens until you're ready."

Hesitantly she curled her fingers around his length. Her eyes widened as she encountered its size and turgidity. Determined to go through with this, she gulped back her fears and slowly drew him to her.

He joined his hand with hers. "It'll help if we

moisten it a little.'' Smiling at the question in her eyes, he dipped his fingers into her moistness, then rubbed what he'd gathered down the length of his shaft.

Shifting slightly, he braced his hands at either side of her head. ''Whenever you're ready.''

She gulped again and nodded, then lifted her hips. She closed her eyes as the tip of his sex pushed against her opening. Then, taking a deep breath, she lifted her hips higher, and he slid inside. She tensed, waiting for the pain. When she felt only pleasure, she opened her eyes to look at him in surprise.

Brushing a lock of hair from her forehead, he lowered his hips, pressing her back against the mattress. ''See?'' he said. ''It doesn't have to hurt.''

Thinking it was over, she stared, wondering what it was that people found so fascinating about sex. Personally she found the whole act rather anticlimactic. Trying her best to hide her disappointment, she nodded.

But instead of rolling off her, as she'd thought he would, he caught her hands and dragged them up the sheets to pin them above her head. ''And now comes the good part,'' he told her.

''What? But—'' Her breath caught in her throat as he pressed his hips against hers and pushed deeper inside. Heat shot through her, stealing her breath and scorching her throat. Her body responded naturally, instinctively, opening for him, then closing around him. But it wasn't enough. She wanted, needed more.

She lifted her hips, straining against the hands that held hers.

But instead of pushing even deeper, giving her what she wanted, he began to slowly withdraw. She vised her knees at his hips, trying to hold him inside. Still, he withdrew. Just when she was sure he intended this as torture of the cruelest kind, he surged forward, and his hips slammed against hers. She arched, rising to meet him, her back bowed, her body straining toward the pleasure.

A sob filled her throat as he slowly withdrew only to plunge again, each thrust faster and deeper than the one before. Nearly crazy with desire, she raced with him, matching him stroke for stroke. Pressure built inside her, seeming to push at her from every direction until she feared she would smother beneath its weight.

When she was sure she would die if he didn't do something to help her, he rammed his hips against hers one last time. With his head thrown back, his teeth clenched, his fingers gripped tightly around hers, he held himself rigid above her, his body a quivering arch of steel molded in the soft satin curve of hers. A low guttural growl rumbled deep inside him, slipped past his clenched teeth. The sound of it, the glorious pressure of his body against hers, set off an explosion inside her, a blinding burst of sensation and color that seemed to sweep her up and toss her high. She closed her eyes and held tightly to his hands, riding the wave of pleasure to its peak.

As if from a distance, she became aware of the slow

melt of his body against hers, the warm, slow rush of his breath at her ear. Choked with emotion, she tugged her hands from his and flung her arms around him, desperate to hold on to the euphoric feeling that filled her.

He curved a hand around the side of her head and turned his face to her cheek. "You okay?"

A smile bloomed inside her and spread slowly across her face. Turning her head to meet his lips, she whispered, "Perfect."

Clay awoke first, just before daylight, opening his eyes and slowly bringing Fiona into focus. She lay facing him, sharing his pillow, one hand curled into a fist beneath her cheek, the fingers of the other splayed loosely across his chest. Her legs were drawn up, her knees tucked into his groin. For a moment he simply stared, remembering.

A virgin, he thought, still unable to comprehend how that could be. She'd had hundreds of boyfriends. Maybe thousands. Yet she'd said, in so many words, that he was the first man she considered worthy of losing her virginity to.

He blew out a shuddery breath as the significance of that confession settled over him.

A virgin, he thought again, and covered the hand she held against his chest, weaving his fingers through hers. And she'd chosen him, Clay Martin, as her first lover. Why? he asked himself, suddenly curious. He wasn't as wealthy or as suave as the guys she must've dated over the years. And he sure as hell hadn't done anything to endear himself to her.

She stirred and the question faded in importance as her knee nudged his lax manhood, urging it to life. He felt himself growing hard and wondered what she'd do if he were to wake her and make love to her again. Would she respond with the same level of passion she'd shown him the night before? Or would morning bring a different response entirely? Would she be horrified when she awoke and realized what they'd done? Would she have regrets?

Of course she would, he told himself. If not now, then later. Deciding he wouldn't wait around to witness her disappointment, he rolled over and sat up, intending to dress and leave before she woke up.

But a hand settled lightly on his back, stopping him before he could stand.

"Clay?"

Her voice, husky with sleep, wrapped itself around his heart and squeezed. "What?"

He felt the thin mattress give beneath him as she crawled to kneel behind him. She wound her arms around his waist and laid her cheek in the middle of his back. "Don't go," she murmured. She turned her lips to his spine. "Please?"

He angled his head to look at her over his shoulder. The smile she offered him was sleepy, sensual.

And he knew he wasn't going anywhere.

She lifted her arms and wrapped them around his neck, drawing him down with her, pillowing his head against her breasts. As she stroked her hands over his back, his mind emptied to all but her soothing touch.

"Clay?"

"Hmm?"

"When were you injured?"

He tensed, feeling her finger trailing along the scar that stretched down his back. "While I was in the service overseas."

"What happened?"

Clay didn't like thinking about that time. The memories were still too fresh, too painful. At times, as debilitating as the tortures themselves he'd endured. More than a year later, and her question had the power to thrust him back into the cramped bamboo cage his captors had imprisoned him in. The oppressive heat, the stench of rotten food and his own excrement, the burning slash of the whip they'd used to try to force him to talk.

He squeezed his eyes shut, forcing the memories back into the deepest recesses of his mind and closing them off.

"I was captured while on a mission."

Her hand froze on his back. "You were tortured?"

He heard the shock in her voice, the horror, and tried to distill it by making light of what had proved to be a life-altering event. "I guess they grew tired of hearing my name, rank and serial number."

For a moment she was silent, still, then he felt the caress of her lips against his hair, the spread of her fingers over his scar, and absorbed the comfort and tenderness in each.

He closed his eyes and burrowed deeper into her warmth. "You amaze me."

"And you disappoint me."

He twisted his head around to look at her in surprise. "Why?"

"You thought your scars would bother me."

He scowled. "You wouldn't have been the first."

Fiona stared, stunned by the feelings of jealousy and indignation that fought for dominance in her heart. "A woman?" she asked before she could stop herself.

He turned away, dropping his head onto her breasts again. "She's not important."

"She is if she was able to hurt you."

"Not any longer."

She caught her lip between her teeth, knowing she shouldn't pry, but unable to stop herself from doing so. "Who was she?"

"Celine Simone, a woman I dated when I was overseas."

She gulped, then asked, "Were you in love with her?"

At first, Fiona didn't think he would answer, then he said in a voice so low she had to strain to hear, "I thought I was. Even wanted to marry her."

"What happened?"

"After my rescue I was in the hospital for a couple of weeks. When I was released, I went to see her and found out she was pregnant."

"Was the baby yours?"

He snorted. "Yeah. It was mine, all right."

She heard the bitterness in his voice and wondered at it, but forced herself to listen as he continued.

"I proposed, but she had other ideas."

"What?" she asked, unable to imagine anyone not wanting to marry Clay.

"She had an abortion."

She heard the regret in his voice, the anger. "Oh, Clay," she murmured. "Why?"

"I can only guess—she never offered an explanation. But I figure it was because of the scars. She couldn't handle imperfections of any kind. Took one look at me and hightailed it outta there. I learned about the abortion later, through friends."

Everything began to make sense to Fiona now. His reluctance to bare his back to her. His rejection of her when she'd discovered them.

She pressed a kiss to his hair again. "And you thought I would react the same as she did to your injuries."

"I wouldn't have blamed you. Still wouldn't."

"Oh, Clay," she said sadly. "I can't believe that you'd think I'm that shallow, that cold."

He lifted his head to look at her. Seeing the hurt in her eyes, he pushed up on an elbow. When she tried to look away, he crooked a finger beneath her chin and held her face before his. "I'm sorry, Fiona. I misjudged you. But I won't make that mistake again," he said. "Promise."

She stared at him, unsure if he was sincere, then threw her arms around his neck and hugged him tightly. "I forgive you."

Chuckling, he slid an arm beneath her waist. "Like I said," he murmured, "you amaze me."

"Better to amaze you than bore you."

He laughed and rolled to his side, snuggling her against his chest. "As if you could ever bore me."

"It's possible," she insisted.

With his gaze on hers, he traced a finger beneath her eye and shook his head. "Never. Not in a million years."

Sunlight flooded the sitting room when Clay awoke the second time. But now he awoke with a start, his heart pounding against his chest, his body bathed in a cold sweat. He stared at Fiona as the thought that had jerked him from sleep screamed through his mind.

He hadn't used any protection. Hadn't even *thought* about the need for protection.

And prior to last night she'd been a virgin, which meant she probably wasn't on the pill. Hell, there wouldn't have been any reason for her to be!

"Clay?"

He glanced over to see that she was awake, too, and was peering at him, her brows drawn together in concern. Realizing that he had a death grip on her hand, he forced his fingers to relax. "Sorry."

"Is something wrong?"

He hesitated, unsure how to resolve his fears without alarming her. He finally decided the direct approach was probably best. "Are you on the pill?"

Her frown deepened. "Yes. For about six months. My gynecologist put me on it to regulate my periods. Why?"

He dropped his forehead against hers, going weak with relief. "Thank God. I didn't think to ask. And I... Never mind."

She pushed away from him and playfully thumped a fist against his head. "And Daddy thinks *I'm* irresponsible," she muttered.

Laughing, he wrapped his arms around her and pulled her back to him. "I'll be sure to tell him you passed the responsible-sex test."

She looked at him in dismay. "You wouldn't!"

Able to tease now that his fears had been put to rest, he arched a brow. "Wouldn't I?" He reached out to twine a stray lock of hair behind her ear, then added, "Of course, first I'd want to retest to verify that my initial findings were correct."

She snuggled close. "Which means you'd have to seduce me, right?"

He heaved a weary sigh. "I suppose so." He leaned over to kiss her, but she slid a hand between their mouths, blocking his kiss.

He drew back and frowned. "What?"

"Would you mind if we moved the test to the bedroom?" She wrinkled her nose. "It seems such a waste to conduct the test here on this flimsy bed when we have all that wonderful technology in the other room.''

Remembering the controller and wondering what other devices it monitored, he rolled from the bed and to his feet, pulling her up with him. "Good idea." He ducked a shoulder into her stomach and lifted her, locking an arm behind her knees.

She squealed, laughing, as he loped to the bedroom, her head bumping against his back.

Nine

They feasted on caviar and champagne, slept, made love, slept some more, then made love again. They argued over what movie to order from the schedule listed on the television, then ended up not ordering a movie at all and made love instead.

They tried out the Jacuzzi, giving each other sensual foot massages that led to more intimate and titillating massages on other body parts. Later, with their arms wrapped around each other's waists, they watched the sun set over the manicured expanse of the golf course from the privacy of their balcony, then turned back into their room and ordered room service.

They talked and laughed while feeding each other shrimp cocktail and broken bits of French bread they'd pinched from a warm loaf provided with their meal. Then they'd shoved aside the cart with the plates of prime rib and steamed vegetables, letting the food grow cold as they crawled back into bed and fed another hunger.

They spent the next day similarly, ordering room service when they were hungry and making love for hours and hours. It was just after ten Sunday night before they were able to drag themselves from bed and dress for the drive home.

Walking with Clay's arm hugged against her side, Fiona stopped in the parking lot at the side of her car. Turning, she smiled up at him and rested her palms against his chest. "I wish we weren't in separate cars."

Though Clay would've sworn his body was too weak to respond to the invitation in her eyes, the sultry tug of her voice, he found himself growing hard, wondering what pleasures she might've had planned for him on the drive home, if they hadn't come to the country club in two cars. He cupped his hands low on her behind, dragged her closer and lowered his head over hers. "Yeah. Me, too."

But before his lips touched hers, a woman's scream rent the air. He jerked his head up, searching the darkness for the source of the sound. He started to pull away, but Fiona tightened her hold on him.

"Don't go," she cried. "The country club has a security officer. If there's a problem, he'll handle it."

Clay opened the door of her Mercedes and urged her behind the wheel. "He may need help," he said, then dropped a quick kiss on her mouth. "Go on home. I'll meet you there as soon as I can."

After locking and closing her door, he ran in the direction he thought the sound had originated. Ducking into the service alley behind the restaurant, he stopped and searched the shadows with his gaze, but saw nothing. A whimper came from a row of Dumpsters, and he ran toward the sound. He found a woman huddled between two of the bins, sobbing, her arms crossed protectively over her head.

He hunkered down in front of her. "Ma'am? Are you hurt?"

She looked up, and the one security light behind Clay revealed terror-filled eyes and a face streaked with tears.

"Ginger?" he said, recognizing the young woman from the spa.

Her sobs rose and she grabbed for him, throwing her arms around his neck and clinging. "Oh, God, Clay!" she cried. "He tried to kill me."

Clay patted her back, trying to calm her. "Who?"

"Pauley. A dishwasher at the club. He ran when he heard you coming."

Clay forced her back to examine her. "Are you hurt?"

She closed a hand around her throat and shook her head, her eyes raw with fear. "No," she said, choking on a sob. "But he had a knife. When I stepped out the back door to take out the garbage, he grabbed me from behind and held the blade against my throat. He said he'd kill me if I didn't tell him about Daisy."

Clay tensed at the name, knowing Ginger was talking about Daisy Parker, a waitress at the Lone Star Country Club. The same waitress the FBI seemed to have an interest in. "Daisy Parker?" he asked, to make sure he had assumed correctly.

She nodded, then collapsed into sobs again. "I

didn't want to tell him,'' she wailed miserably, ''but I was so afraid.''

''Tell him what?''

''That Daisy is Baby Lena's mother.''

Clay slowly absorbed the importance of the confession as he drew her to her feet. ''Let's get you inside,'' he said, guiding her toward the back door of the restaurant, ''then I'll call the police.''

While Clay listened to Ginger repeat her story for the police, in another alley across town Pauley was telling Erica Clawson his own version of the mugging.

''I swear,'' he said, his breath coming in hard gasps. ''That's exactly what she said. Daisy's the brat's mother.'' He glanced nervously around and stuck out his hand. ''Now give me the money. I gotta split, 'fore the cops come looking for me.''

Erica pressed a wad of bills into his hand. ''Remember, Pauley,'' she warned. ''I had nothing to do with this.''

''Yeah, yeah,'' he muttered, quickly palming the money. ''If I swing, I swing alone.''

''Exactly,'' she murmured, as she watched him duck into the shadows. She waited until the sound of his footsteps faded, then stepped from the alley and entered the apartment building. Once inside the elevator and on her way to the top floor, she pulled a small container of perfume from her shoulder bag and spritzed behind her ears, between her breasts and up under her skirt. Obsession. It was Frank's favorite fragrance.

All but giddy with excitement, she stepped from the elevator and used her key to unlock the door. As she closed it behind her, Frank looked up from the bar. Frowning, he finished pouring his drink.

"This better be good," he warned. He lifted the glass, tossed the vodka back, then narrowed an eye at her. "You know I hate having my string jerked by some female."

Erica stared, growing wet just looking at him. Frank Del Brio was everything she'd ever wanted in a man. Handsome, wealthy, powerful. She'd had a crush on him for years, slept with him for the past two. She was sure that with this bit of information she would prove her loyalty to him and earn herself an engagement ring.

With her gaze on his, she let her bag slide off her shoulder and started toward him, slowing unbuttoning her blouse. "There's only one string of yours I'm interested in pulling, Frank." Reaching him, she lifted her arms and wrapped them around his neck. She flicked her tongue at his lips and rubbed her bare breasts across his chest. She smiled, pleased, when he groaned and thrust his hips hard against her abdomen.

His ability to go from zero to horny in a nanosecond was just another reason she loved Frank so much. Laughing, she pushed her hands against his chest. "Hold it, Italian Stallion. I've got some news you're gonna want to hear."

He filled his hands with her buttocks and lifted her, holding her against him as he crossed to the sofa. "The only thing I want to hear is you screaming for more." He dropped her to the sofa and followed her down, burying his face between her breasts as he fought to free his sex.

"Oh, you'll want to hear this," she told him. "Daisy is Baby Lena's mother."

He froze, then pushed back to look at her. "How do you know?"

"Ginger. Daisy told her, but swore her to secrecy."

"And the chick just spills her guts to you?" He snorted and jerked up his zipper. "What—you take me for some kind of fool?"

"No!" she cried, desperate to make him believe her. "Ginger didn't tell me. She told Pauley, a dishwasher at the country club. I knew she had to know something, so I paid him to get her to talk."

He eyed her suspiciously a moment, then swooped down to kiss her with a fierceness that stole her breath. When he drew back, he was grinning from ear to ear. "So, did Ginger verify that Daisy is really Haley Mercado?"

"What?" she asked dully.

"Did Ginger verify that Daisy is really Haley?" he repeated, then frowned. "You did tell Pauley to find that out, too, didn't you?"

She shook her head. "Well, no. I just thought you wanted to know if Daisy was Lena's mother."

He rolled off her and to his feet. "You stupid

bitch!'' He opened his hand and slapped her hard across the face. The whack of flesh striking flesh echoed viciously in the suddenly quiet room.

"I don't give a damn about the baby!" he shouted. "My only interest in the brat is if Haley is her mother."

Her ears ringing from the slap, Erica struggled to sit up. "I'll find out," she promised.

"How? You gonna just walk up to her at work and say, 'Oh, by the way, Daisy, are you really Haley Mercado?'" Swearing, he snatched a vase from the end table and hurled it at the wall.

Erica cringed as it exploded, shooting shards of glass halfway across the room. She eased to her feet and moved toward him, knowing she had to calm him down before he destroyed everything in her apartment. "We'll kidnap her," she said.

He whipped his head around to frown at her. "Kidnap Daisy?"

"No," she said, relieved that she had succeeded in distracting him from his rage, and even more relieved that he hadn't hit her again. "The baby. We can snatch her right off Carson ranch. If we do, and Daisy is really Haley, then she'll be forced out of hiding."

Frank's eyes narrowed as he considered the plan.

Erica knew how to convince him to see things her way. She crossed to him and cupped him with her hand. "If anybody can steal something right out from under the Carsons' noses, you can." She rubbed her breasts against his chest. "You're so smart, Frank.

That's just one of the reasons why I'm so crazy about you.'' She squeezed her fingers around his quickly hardening arousal and smiled as she pressed herself closer to him. "This is another.''

By the time Clay reached the ranch, it was well after midnight. He'd hoped to find Fiona waiting up for him and bit back his disappointment when he found the windows dark, the house quiet as a tomb. He hesitated at her closed bedroom door, wanting more than anything to slip inside, crawl into bed with her and pick up from where they'd left off in the parking lot. But doubts crowded his mind, keeping him from reaching for the knob. Would she still want him? Or had she, in the hours they'd been apart, realized that she'd made a mistake and now regretted having slept with him?

Unsure of his reception, he turned away and continued on to his room. By the time he reached it, he'd convinced himself that the entire weekend had been nothing more than a dream, a moment stolen out of time. The luxurious fantasy suite, with all its soft candlelight and romantic music, had seduced them both into believing they were really husband and wife, and they'd succumbed to its spell.

Depressed by the thought, he didn't bother turning on the light, but dropped his suit jacket on the floor and tugged his shirttail from the waist of his slacks as he crossed to the bed. Shrugging off his shirt, he unfastened the waist of his slacks one-handed, while peeling back the covers with the other. Just as he reached for his zipper, the overhead light flashed on. He whirled, throwing up a hand to shade his eyes.

Fiona stood in the doorway, her hand poised over the light switch, her curves a seductive silhouette beneath a silk-and-lace gown the color of a summer sky. Her hair, mussed from sleep, hung past her shoulders. One strand curled above her right breast, looking like an upside-down question mark against her porcelain skin.

She lifted a brow. "Is the light too bright?"

He dropped his hand to his side and shook his head. "No. Just took a minute for my eyes to adjust."

She dragged a finger over the switch, plunging the room into darkness again. It took another moment for his eyes to readjust to the change. By the time they did, she had moved and was now standing directly in front of him, an ethereal shadow of pulsing sensuality and erotic scents that swirled around him and clouded his brain.

"Was everything okay at the club?"

He prayed that she would touch him, absolve the doubts that kept him from reaching out for her. When she didn't, he said, "One of the waitresses was mugged. Ginger Walton," he clarified. "Some guy put a knife to her throat."

"Oh, my God," Fiona said, sounding truly concerned. "Was she hurt?"

"No. Just shook up pretty bad."

"Did you catch the guy?"

"No. By the time I got to her, he was gone. She was able to identify him, though. The police have already picked him up."

She stepped closer, so close he could feel the warmth of her body, a wave of heat surging against his.

"That's good," she murmured softly. "I'm sure she'll sleep better knowing her attacker is behind bars."

"Fiona," he began, wishing to God he had the courage to touch her, to make that first move.

She eased closer, her face tipped up expectantly to his. "Yes?"

It was then that he saw the uncertainty in her eyes, the same doubts that he was sure were mirrored in his. He caught her elbows and drew her against him, wrapping his arms around hers. "Oh, Fiona," he said, releasing a shaky breath. "I was afraid..."

She pulled back to look up at him. "Afraid of what?"

He laughed softly, embarrassed to admit his fears. "Nothing, really. It was just that I thought that you...well, that you might've had second thoughts. Regrets," he added cautiously.

She moved her hands to frame his face. "I thought the same of you," she admitted. "I heard you stop at my door, but when you didn't come in, I was convinced that you regretted our weekend together."

He slid his arms down her back and locked them

behind her waist. "The only regret I have is that I couldn't come home with you."

Smiling, she looped her arms around his neck. "You're home now," she reminded him.

He grinned. "Yeah, so I am. Are you tired?"

"No. Are you?"

"Uh-uh." He rubbed his groin across hers. "My bed isn't equipped with any of those technological wonders like the one at the club, but it's comfortable and there's plenty of room for two."

She arched a brow. "Is that an invitation?"

He lowered his head over hers. "Yeah," he said, the admission a lustful sigh against her lips. "Are you accepting?"

The next morning Clay sat huddled with a group of FBI agents around a scarred table in an abandoned office of what had once been a thriving stone-cutting company on the edge of town. The business had gone under years before, and the FBI had commandeered the deteriorating building to use as a temporary control center, while they conducted their investigation of the Mayan artifacts being smuggled across the border from Mexico.

The men were a motley group, each bringing to the investigative team their own special talents. One, a man with international connections throughout the art world, looked more like a migrant farm worker than a highly renowned archeologist with a specialty in Mayan artifacts. But that was part of the plan. None of the men wanted to be recognized. Couldn't afford to be. To do so would not only jeopardize the success of the investigation, but their safety, as well.

Clay wasn't an official member of the team, but the men had called on him before when they needed information quickly, relying on his familiarity with the geography of the area and his knowledge of the townspeople.

Sean Collins, the agent in charge, shifted his gaze to Clay. "We understand that you were the first person on the scene when the waitress was mugged at the country club."

Clay nodded. "Ginger Walton," he said, supplying the woman's name. "She was pretty shook up, but suffered no physical injuries, other than a bruise or two."

"Do you know anything about her attacker?" another asked.

"Some. His name's Pauley Rucker. He's currently employed as a dishwasher at the country club, although he had a string of other jobs before this one. Basically he's a drifter with an expensive drug habit. Nothing that's gotten him in serious trouble," he was quick to add. "Just petty stuff that's earned him some jail time."

"Do you think he's involved in the smuggling ring?" one of the agents asked.

Clay pursed his lips, giving the question the consideration it deserved, then shook his head. "They'd never let him into the fold. He's too big a screwup."

He huffed a laugh. "Hell, when he left the restaurant, he left a trail a blind man could have followed. And when the police hauled him in, he sang like a canary, letting them know real quick that the mugging wasn't his idea. Swore he was hired by Erica Clawson to attack Ginger."

"Erica Clawson?" one of the men asked in surprise. "The chick who's been sleeping with Frank Del Brio?"

"One and the same," Clay confirmed. "According to Pauley, Erica's had her heart set on becoming Mrs. Del Brio for some time. Now that Frank's the official head of the mob, she was looking for a way to endear herself to him a little more. She knew Frank was interested in Daisy, and that Ginger and Daisy had become friends. So she hired Pauley to pry what information he could from Ginger about Daisy so that she could carry it to Frank."

At the mention of Daisy, the men around the table exchanged looks. Clay had suspected for some time that the agents had a connection of some kind with Daisy, one that had made him wonder before if she wasn't a part of their team. He'd never asked, and they'd never offered any information. Which didn't surprise him. The more people they included in their plans, the greater the chance of a leak. And leaks got people killed.

Having delivered the information they'd requested, Clay pushed to his feet and put on his hat. "I better get going. If y'all need anything else, just give me a shout.''

The leader stood and stuck out a hand. "We appreciate the help, Clay.''

Clay shook the offered hand. "Watch your backs,'' he warned. "These guys play dirty. They've killed before and won't hesitate to kill again.''

Sean Collins waited until the door closed behind Clay, then sat again and rested his arms on the scarred table, his expression grim. "Looks as if we're going to have to escalate our plans a bit.'' He turned to the man on his right. "Can you arrange to have Daisy wired with the miniature tape recorder again?''

The agent grinned. "Sure thing, boss. It's still in the trunk of my car.''

"Good. Let's hope she can keep her identity a secret a little longer. At least until she's able to get the information we need to nail the mob.''

Fiona moved from the den to the hallway, dragging the upright vacuum cleaner behind her and humming the tune to "Unforgettable,'' one of the tunes she and Clay had danced to at the reception. As she stooped to plug the cord into the wall outlet beneath a window, she caught a glimpse of her reflection in the glass and sputtered a laugh.

"Oh, if Anita could see me now,'' she said, patting at the bandanna she'd wrapped around her head.

Laughing, she straightened, switched on the vacuum and began to push it over the carpet.

If anyone had questioned her, she couldn't have explained this sudden burst of domesticity. All she knew was that she'd awakened feeling more energized than she had in years. With no other outlet for her energy, she'd decided to clean house.

She had never cleaned house before, but she'd spent enough hours visiting with Anita while Anita went about her chores at the Carson estate that she had a fairly good idea what was required. She'd started by sweeping and mopping the kitchen floor, then wiped down all the countertops and washed and put away the cereal bowls left from her and Clay's breakfast. With energy still to burn, she'd moved on to the den, vacuuming the carpet and dusting all the furniture.

She made the last swipe down the hallway and switched off the vacuum. Done, she thought proudly. What next? She eyed the closed door opposite her, knowing that behind it was Clay's home office. Should she clean there, as well, before attacking the bedrooms? He'd never invited her into his office and kept the door closed at all times. She tried the knob and it turned in her hand. With a shrug she opened the door and walked in.

Boxes, stacked two and three deep, lined the walls. In the center of the room stood a gunmetal-gray desk, its top cluttered with a wild assortment of papers and files. A phone cord stretched from a wall outlet to a generic black phone propped on top of a telephone directory, both shoved to a far corner of the desk. Another cord led to a fax machine perched atop a box. Wads of paper littered the floor and overflowed a wastebasket.

"Heavens," she murmured, unsure where to begin. "What a mess."

Blowing out a breath, she crossed to the wastebasket and mashed down its contents, then started picking up the wads of paper and dropping them inside. Once done, she moved on to the desk, careful not to trip on the phone cord. She frowned at the clutter of paper and files scattered across the desktop, then pulled up the chair, sat down and began to shuffle them into separate groups. Folders went into one pile, loose papers into another, unopened mail into a third. It wasn't much of a filing system, but she figured it was better than the disarray Clay had left behind.

When she'd finished, she stood, ready to vacuum. But as she turned, she inadvertently bumped the desk, and the tall stack of file folders began to teeter. With a cry of alarm, she lunged, wrapping her arms around the files and catching the bulk of them before they all slid to the floor.

With a sigh of relief she straightened the stack, then circled the desk and knelt to gather the fallen folders. Papers had slid from one and she quickly pushed them back inside and started to rise. As she did, she noticed a photograph lying on the floor. Shifting the folders to hold against her chest, she bent to scoop it up.

The folders slid to the floor forgotten as she stared

at the child pictured there. "Oh, my God," she moaned, gulping back the nausea that pushed at her throat. Bonelessly she moved back around the desk and sank onto the chair, her gaze riveted to the child's broken and twisted body. Lifeless eyes stared back at her from a bruised and bloody face. A girl, she realized, noting the long blond hair matted with dried blood. She couldn't be more than seven or eight.

Tears burned her eyes, stung her throat. She clapped a hand over her mouth to smother the sob that climbed higher with each gasped breath. But she couldn't look away. Even when tears blurred the image, the horror of it held her rooted to Clay's chair, her gaze frozen on the picture gripped tightly in her hand.

Clay found her there less than an hour later, her fingers still pressed against her mouth, her face pale, her eyes fixed on the picture she held.

Without looking, he knew what she'd found. He bolted across the room and dropped down at her side. "Fiona," he said softly, easing the photo from her stiff fingers. "Let go, honey. You don't need to see this."

He tossed the picture aside and pulled her hand away from her mouth, gathering them both within his own. Her skin was cold, icy, her fingers stiff. "Fiona," he said gently.

She turned her head slowly to look at him, but he wondered if she saw him at all, her eyes were so glazed.

"Fiona," he said more urgently, chafing her hands between his.

Slowly she focused on him. Her lip trembled and her eyes filled with tears. "Clay?"

Her voice was scratchy, nothing but a hoarse whisper. She sounded as if she'd been screaming for hours. He wondered if she had.

Anxious to get her out of the room and as far away from the picture as he could, he caught her beneath the knees and stood, swinging her up into his arms. He strode for the door and out into the hall, his only thought to get her outside. Sunshine and fresh air. That was what she needed.

"Clay?"

"Shh," he soothed, shouldering open the door and stepping out onto the front porch. He sat down on the top step and held her on his lap, cradled against his chest. He felt the trembles that shook her body, the clammy chill of her skin, and wished to God he'd had the good sense to put a lock on the office door.

He hugged her more closely to his chest, trying to warm her, then pressed his lips to the top of her head.

"I'm sorry, Fiona," he murmured. "You shouldn't have had to see that. No one should."

She hiccuped a sob and turned her face into his chest. "Oh, Clay," she cried softly. "She was so young."

He set his jaw, knowing too well the details of the case. "Yeah, I know."

She curled her hands into fists against his chest and

pushed back to look at him, her face streaked with tears. "What kind of person would do that to a little girl?"

He fixed his mouth in a grim line and looked away, knowing that any explanation he offered wouldn't come close to describing the man who'd brutally raped and murdered the girl. "A very sick man," was all he said.

He felt her gaze on his face, sensed in the tightening of her fists against his chest her realization of exactly what kind of man would prey on a young girl and all that man had done to the child.

"Where were her parents?"

He glanced at her, then away again, narrowing his eyes at the pastures. "Parent," he corrected. "Her mother was raising her alone. Her father skipped out on them years ago."

"Well, where was her mother, then? She should've been taking care of her. Protecting her."

He heard the anger in her voice, the accusation. He might've reacted in much the same way if he hadn't met the girl's mother, spent hours trying to console the grief-stricken, guilt-ridden woman. "She was at work."

Fiona shot off his lap and whirled to face him, her hands balled at her sides. "Do you mean to tell me that she left that poor baby all alone?"

He heaved a sigh. "It's not that simple, Fiona. She—"

"It *is* that simple," she cried, cutting him off. "She

was her *mother,* for God's sake, and responsible for the child's safety.''

Something inside Clay snapped. He stood and shoved his face in front of hers. ''Not everyone is lucky enough to live the same privileged lifestyle as you.''

She drew back, looking wounded. ''What do you mean?''

''Hell, Fiona,'' he said, gesturing wildly, ''that woman lives at the poverty level. She was putting in twelve-hour days just to keep a roof over their heads and food on their table.''

''She should have arranged for child care. No child should be left alone.''

''And how was she supposed to pay for it?'' he returned. ''Child care costs money. Money she didn't have.''

''Surely there are agencies,'' she began.

''There aren't.''

''Programs for single mothers?''

''Nope.''

Her anger returned, staining her cheeks a dark red, setting her eyes aflame. ''Well, there should be. If the government can find the funds to send a man to the moon, then it should be able to provide child care for parents who can't afford it.''

''Why put the responsibility on the government?''

''Well, somebody should do something!''

He folded his arms across his chest. ''Yeah, somebody should.''

She drew back. "Why are you looking at me that way?"

"What way?"

"As if I'm that somebody."

"What else have you got to do with your time?"

She pushed out a hand, backing away from him. "Uh-uh. Not me. I wouldn't know where to begin."

He dropped back his head and laughed.

She stopped to peer at him. "What are you laughing at?"

"You. You've spent your entire life getting people to do what you want. Why not put that skill to good use for a change?"

"I don't know what you mean."

He caught her hand and drew her back to the steps, tugging her down to sit beside him. "It's not as if you have to take on world hunger. Start right here in Mission Creek. You've got the contacts. You know the people with the money. Hit 'em up for a donation to build a child-care facility right here in your own hometown."

She didn't say anything, just stared at him, but he could almost hear the wheels churning.

He slung an arm around her shoulders and hugged her against his side. "You can do it. I know you can."

"I could, couldn't I," she said slowly.

"It's just a matter of setting your mind to the task."

She rose, chewing thoughtfully at her thumbnail. "I'll need to make a list of possible donors. I can start with the country-club roster. Flynt can get me a copy."

"Now you're talking," he said.

"We'll need land for the building. Daddy should have something he'd be willing to donate."

"If he doesn't, he'd know who would."

"Yeah," she said, her eyes growing bright with excitement. "And whatever Daddy gives, you know the Wainrights will match. They won't want the Carsons showing them up. We'll need a name," she said, and frowned.

"I'm sure you'll come up with a good one."

She charged for the house. "I need paper and pen."

Clay hopped up to follow. "I'll get it for you."

"We may need to add another couple of phone lines," she called over her shoulder.

He paused at the door, frowning at her back. "What for?"

She turned and caught his hand, tugging him inside with her. "For the telethon, silly. That's how all the stars raise money for their favorite charities."

Ten

Clay wasn't sure, but he was afraid he'd created a monster. His entire house had been converted into an office for Fiona's campaign to raise money for the child-care center. She'd yet to settle on a name for the organization, but that hadn't stopped her from getting started. She'd approached the project like a scientist, carefully gathering data and fighting her way through miles of red tape. The proof of her efforts was stacked in neatly labeled piles all over his house. He had managed to persuade her to hold off on the additional phone lines for a while. But he was already questioning his interference. Every time he tried to call home now, he got a busy signal.

Meanwhile Fiona was coming into her own. He never found her stretched out on the sofa any longer, her eyes bleary from watching television all day. And not once since she'd started her campaign had she complained of boredom. She rose early, went to bed late. In the hours between she was either on the phone or visiting child-care facilities around the state.

She was a woman with a mission.

And Clay was a man who suddenly found himself

missing his wife—a wife who was supposed to be nothing more to him than a job.

When had his feelings for her changed? he wondered. From the beginning he'd considered Fiona spoiled, selfish, her behavior juvenile, erratic, destructive. But somewhere along the way, his opinion of her had changed...or *she'd* changed. She was happier, less volatile, thought less about herself and her own needs. He couldn't really say that she was calmer than before, because she had attacked this child-care center idea with a fierceness that had her charging around as if the facility had to be built overnight.

He supposed he understood what possessed her. The photo of that little girl was hard to forget. In Fiona's mind, he was sure, she felt she had to do something before another child was harmed, another life lost. Clay had felt that way himself the first time he'd stood over a victim of a crime. Still did, if he was honest with himself. It was the memory of that horror, that waste, that kept him on the job long after the five-o'clock whistle blew. It was what fed his determination to sweep all the riffraff and thugs from town. It was what made him want to make Mission Creek a safe town to live in again. More like the town in which he'd grown up.

Clay chose a stool at the bar in the Men's Grill and slid onto it, knowing that the mirror behind the bar offered him the best—and most discreet—view of the activity in the room. He ordered a club sandwich and a beer, but not because he was hungry. His purpose in ordering the food was only a cover. Sean Collins, the FBI leader, had contacted him earlier in the day and asked him to drop by the grill and serve as their eyes and ears. He'd also asked Clay to do what he could to protect Daisy, if the plan they'd outlined didn't go down as they'd hoped.

At four o'clock in the afternoon, the Men's Grill wasn't all that busy. A couple of golfers sat at the other end of the bar, analyzing, over a couple of beers, the swings and putts they'd made during their game. The clack of balls coming from the Billiard Room let Clay know that there were a few customers in there, as well. But it was the four men huddled in a booth in a far corner of the room that held his interest. Frank Del Brio and three of his gang, he thought with a shake of his head. It never ceased to amaze him that they would choose such a public place for their meetings.

As he sipped his beer, Clay kept one eye on the booth where the gang sat and another on Daisy, who was working her way toward the booth, pretending to clean tables and refill salt and pepper shakers for the evening's rush of dinner guests. He gave her a quick once-over, but was unable to detect any sign of the recorder Collins had told him they'd wired her with. He prayed, for her sake, that the mob guys weren't able to detect it, either.

The bartender placed a plate in front of Clay, and Clay mumbled his thanks, then spread the linen napkin across his lap. He picked up the sandwich and took a bite, but kept his gaze on the mirror. As he watched, he saw Daisy approach the booth to refill the men's cups of coffee. Though he couldn't see Daisy's face, he had a clear view of Frank's, and the hate that filled Frank's eyes as he looked at her made Clay's skin crawl.

Daisy left the table and returned to her duties, stripping off the linen cloth on the table next to the booth. With a calmness that amazed Clay, she spread a clean one over the top, then began to set out silver and glasses. But always with her left shoulder turned toward Frank's booth. Clay bit back a smile. Obviously the recorder had been concealed underneath the left side of her shirt, probably in her bra.

He polished off the sandwich and was considering ordering something for dessert, to give him an excuse to hang around a little longer, when he saw Daisy head for the back hallway and the rest rooms located there. When she returned, she picked up the tray that held the large containers of salt and pepper that she'd used to refill the shakers and headed for the bar. She placed the containers in a storage cabinet beneath the sink, then picked up a cloth and began to wipe down the bar.

When she reached Clay, she glanced his way and smiled. "Can I get you something else, Ranger Martin?"

"I was considering having some dessert. What would you recommend?"

"The apple pie seems to be everyone's favorite, though, personally, I prefer the cheesecake."

He shoved aside his empty plate. "Cheesecake it'll be, then."

She moved to the end of the bar, removed a cheesecake from a glass-fronted refrigerator and arranged a slice on a plate. When she returned, she set the plate in front of him and looked directly into his eyes. "I hope you enjoy the cheesecake. It's topped with fresh cherries, so you might want to watch out for stray pits."

Puzzled by the strange warning, as well as the intensity of her gaze, Clay picked up his fork and sliced into the dessert. He'd consumed three bites when his fork struck something hard. He had to quickly school his features as he moved the utensil through the cheesecake and discovered the cassette. Realizing that Daisy must have obtained the information the FBI needed, he glanced at the mirror to make sure that Frank and his buddies weren't looking, then slid the cassette into his napkin and onto his hand, closing his fingers around it.

Rising, he pushed his fist into his pocket and reached for his hat. "Thanks, Daisy," he called as he pulled on his hat. "The cheesecake was delicious."

"You're welcome, Ranger Martin," she replied with a bright smile. "Come back and see us again soon."

Clay sat with the agents huddled around the table, listening to the tape.

"Stop and back it up a little," Collins ordered. "And see if you can get rid of some of that background noise," he added, frowning.

The man operating the hi-tech sound equipment punched a few buttons, twirled some knobs, and the tape began to play again. All the men leaned forward, their foreheads knotted in concentration. When the tape ended, they sank back in their chairs with a collective sigh of relief.

"Well, she did it," Collins said proudly. "Daisy's provided us with the date and location for the mob's next shipment of smuggled goods."

He turned to Clay then, his expression changing to one of concern. "Do you think they suspected anything?"

Clay shook his head. "No. That woman's got nerves of steel. She worked her way right up to their booth, and they never suspected for a minute that she was doing anything but cleaning tables. But I'll tell you one thing," he added. "Frank Del Brio has it in for her. If you could have seen the way he looked at her when she was refilling their coffee cups..." He shook his head, the memory alone curdling his blood. "Y'all need to do everything you can to protect her. If Frank discovers that Daisy's really Haley Mercado, she's as good as dead."

The FBI leader nodded grimly. "She won't need to worry about Frank much longer. Once the bust is over and we have Frank and the rest of his thugs under arrest, she can drop the assumed identity and get on with her life.''

Clay rose to leave. ''I just hope she lives that long.''

Clay brought his cell phone to his ear. ''Martin,'' he said.

''What's all this nonsense I hear about Fiona wanting land for some child-care center?''

Clay bit back a smile at the grumpiness in Carson's voice. ''It's not nonsense,'' he replied. ''She wants to build a facility for the benefit of single parents who can't afford to pay for child care.''

''And she wants *me* to give her the land?'' he asked, his voice rising.

''Yes, sir,'' Clay replied, holding the phone away from his ear. ''She mentioned that she was going to ask you.''

''Well, she didn't ask me. Flynt told me about it. And I'll be damned if I'll deed over to her a prime piece of land for some harebrained scheme she'll lose interest in before the week is up.''

''She'll be disappointed to hear that, I'm sure,'' Clay replied, trying to keep the amusement from his voice. ''But she's got a backup plan ready, in the event you turned her down.''

''Backup plan,'' Carson repeated. ''What kind of backup plan?''

''Well, I believe I remember her saying something about a piece of property the Wainwrights own near the downtown area.''

"The Wainwrights!"

Wincing, Clay jerked the phone to arm's length, then slowly brought it back to his ear when he was sure that Carson was through yelling.

"Yes, sir. She did her research, choosing sites located near the schools, then prioritized them according to their overall suitability."

"I know what lot of Wainwright's she's thinking of, and I can tell you right now that my lot is a damn sight better than his."

It was all Clay could do not to laugh. "Yes, sir. I believe that's why she intended to approach you first."

"Well, you tell her to call me, you hear? Wainwright will stick some big-ass price tag on his piece of property, just because Fiona is a Carson and has shown some interest in it. I won't let her be taken to the cleaners by an old cuss like Archie Wainwright. No siree, I sure won't. Not when I've got a better piece of property that I'm willing to give to her free and clear."

"I'll give her the message," Clay promised, then disconnected the call. He laughed long and hard, knowing that Ford Carson had played right into his daughter's hands, exactly as Fiona had said he would. She'd thrown out the bait to Flynt, knowing her brother would tell their father of her plans, then had waited for her father to bite.

Now it was just a matter of her reeling him in.

Clay stepped into the house and hooked his hat over the rack by the door. "Fiona?"

"In here," she called.

Clay headed for the den. "If you're hungry, I thought we might go out for—" He stumbled to a stop, his eyes rounding in shock. Fiona sat in the middle of the floor, surrounded by mountains of torn wrapping paper, ribbon and piles of gifts yet to be unwrapped.

"Look," she said, all but beaming as she held up a stainless steel toaster. "Isn't this neat?"

He walked slowly toward her. "What is all this stuff?"

"Wedding gifts!" she replied, laughing gaily. "Since we didn't send out formal announcements, no one knew our address, so they've been sending them to Mother and Daddy's house, and Mother had one of the hands at the ranch deliver them here this afternoon."

Dread twisted in his gut. "Wedding gifts?" he repeated. "But why would people send gifts when we didn't have a wedding?"

"Wedding or not, we're married," she reminded him. "And the gifts are a way for people to offer their good wishes and to show their support. Look at this," she said, holding up a crystal vase. "It's from the staff at the country club. And this," she said, setting down the vase to hold up a large sterling silver bowl, "is from the bank. Isn't it gorgeous?"

Yeah, it was gorgeous, all right, Clay thought, and had probably cost a small fortune.

"And wait until you see this," she said, digging

through the mounds of paper and coming up with a leather-bound photo album. She pushed aside some scraps of paper and ribbon and patted the floor next to her.

Though he really didn't want to see any more, Clay sank down to sit cross-legged beside her.

"It's from Mother and Daddy," she said as she opened the album over their almost touching knees.

The photo secured behind the plastic sleeve hit Clay right square in the heart. It was an eight-by-ten glossy of him and Fiona dancing at the reception. She had one hand looped around his neck, the other resting against his chest. They both had their eyes closed, and her cheek was pressed tightly to his. He remembered the moment almost to the second. They had just begun dancing to "Unforgettable" and Fiona had lifted her head to whisper thank-you in his ear.

"I had forgotten there was a photographer at the reception," he said.

"Since we didn't have a traditional wedding, Mother wanted the reception photographed so that we would have something to commemorate the event."

She turned the page and emotion filled his throat as a picture of Fiona came into view. She was standing beside the fountain in the garden outside the Empire Room. She had one hand braced on the lip of the large, marble basin, and the other was caught mid-toss. A shiny copper penny hung suspended in the air inches from her fingertips.

"That was taken before you arrived," she explained. "It's a tradition at the club that every new bride must make a wish and toss a penny into the fountain."

Without realizing he intended to voice the question, he heard himself asking, "And what was your wish?"

"Happiness," she replied without hesitation. She glanced over at him and smiled. "That's what all the brides wish for."

Clay stared, both humbled and stunned by the simplicity of her wish. He lifted a hand and pushed her hair back from her face. "Are you happy, Fiona?"

Her expression turned curious. "Well, of course I am. Aren't you?"

He was. Far more than he'd ever expected to be. Yet he felt a sudden unease at the realization. One that bordered close to guilt. Their marriage wasn't a real marriage, he reminded himself, not in the true sense of the word. Her father had paid him to marry Fiona, then threatened Fiona with poverty to get her to go along with the deal. What kind of basis was that for a marriage? What kind of hope for the future did a marriage based on greed and fear offer to the two forced into the union?

"Clay?" She tipped her head to peer at him, concern creasing her brow. "You are happy, aren't you?"

He gave himself a shake. "Yeah," he said, and knew at least that much wasn't a lie. "I'm happy."

A smile wreathed her face. "Good." She set the album aside, then shifted to her knees in front of him. "And to answer your question about whether I'm hungry or not..." She looped her arms around his neck and pushed her face close to his. "Only for you."

Clay stared into her eyes, his throat closing up at the sincerity he found in the green depths, the passion. He loved her. The realization hit him with a swiftness, a sureness that would have knocked him over if he hadn't already been sitting on the floor. He gripped her waist and sank back, wrapping paper crinkling beneath him as he pulled her over him.

"I think I know how to satisfy that hunger." He reached for the top button of her blouse. "But first we need to get rid of some of these clothes."

Later that night Clay lay in bed on his side, one hand pillowing his head, the other resting on his thigh, staring at Fiona and reflecting on their activities earlier that evening. They'd made love on the den floor on a bed of crumpled wrapping paper. Afterward she had put on his shirt and insisted on opening the remaining packages. He'd watched, a satin ribbon tied around his neck and a scrap of white wrapping paper embossed with silver wedding bells covering the most telling part of his anatomy. Fiona had tied the ribbon around his neck, laughing as she'd plumped the bow. The paper he'd donned himself, because he'd felt ridiculous lying there buck naked while she was covered from neck to knee by his shirt.

She'd oohed and ahhed over every gift, her pleasure obvious. But each present she'd unveiled only sank

Clay deeper and deeper into a gloom he was only beginning to understand.

He had to end the marriage.

He'd known from the start that their marriage was only temporary, but somewhere along the way he'd lost sight of that fact. Two months, he remembered thinking on the drive back from Mexico. Two months and he could divorce her and get on with his life.

Well, the two-month deadline was still a few weeks away, yet he knew he couldn't wait until then to end their marriage. If he waited, one of them would be hurt, and he didn't mind admitting, if only to himself, that he was the one who'd be hurt the most. Fiona had changed during their weeks together. She wasn't the same selfish, irresponsible woman he'd agreed to marry. She was generous, loving and committed to helping others less fortunate than herself.

And she had displayed uncanny business sense while working to establish the child-care center, one that made him aware that she had only just begun to tap into her real potential. It wouldn't be long before she would realize the mistake she'd made in agreeing to marry him. She'd want to take on more projects, more responsibilities, spread her wings a little. He could see her in a corporate boardroom, going head-to-head with industry giants for her causes. She'd schmooze them over cocktails and dinners, persuading them to put their financial muscle behind her charitable organization. It wouldn't be long before she realized just how much she'd shortchanged herself by marrying Clay. It was only natural that she would compare Clay to the successful businessmen she met with and she'd realize the life she might've had if she hadn't knuckled under to her father's threats and married Clay.

She'd grow to resent him, perhaps eventually hate him. Then she would leave. It would break his heart. He knew that. But was it worse to have it broken sooner, rather than later? If he let her go now, it would be less painful…at least for her.

As he watched her sleep, he had the strongest urge to reach out and gather her into his arms, wanting to store up as many memories as he could for the lonely nights ahead.

But he didn't. He feared if he dared even so much as a touch, he'd never let her go.

After interviewing an inmate at the state prison, one who had told the warden he had information that would be helpful to Clay on a case he was working on, Clay climbed back into his truck and headed for Mission Creek. The drive gave him time to think about the decision he'd made the night before.

He soon realized that ending the marriage wasn't going to be as simple as he'd once thought. First, there was the matter of the money Carson had paid him. Though Clay hadn't come close to spending it all, he had withdrawn a sizable chunk to pay for supplies and equipment he'd bought for the ranch. He'd have to repay the money, he knew, but he didn't want to approach Carson with his plan to divorce Fiona until he had in his hands the full one hundred thousand dollars Carson had paid him. Which presented a problem, because it would take Clay months, maybe even years, to come up with the money.

As he tried to think of a way to raise it, he passed by the Wagner farm, where former district attorney Spence Harrison lived with his new wife, Ellen. A half mile down the road, he slammed on the brakes and whipped the steering to the right, spinning the truck around to head back in the direction he'd just come.

He'd ask Spence to lend him the money, he told himself. No, not lend, he amended quickly, though Spence could well afford to give him the money if he chose to do so. But Clay didn't want to be indebted to anyone ever again. He'd offer Spence a part of the ranch in exchange for the money he owed to Carson, he decided, plus what funds he'd need to complete the repairs. It was a fair deal for both parties.

He turned into the entrance to the farm just as Spence stepped from a barn not far from the house. Clay bumped the heel of his hand against the horn, and Spence glanced up, shading his eyes with a hand. Clay was surprised to see Spence dressed in overalls, instead of the customary three-piece suit he wore when he had served as Mission Creek's district attorney. Marveling at the changes in Spence that had transpired since that fateful day when he'd tangled with a tornado and ended up with amnesia, Clay climbed down from his truck.

"Hey, Clay," Spence called, heading toward him. "What brings you out this way?"

Clay hooked a thumb over his shoulder. "I was at the prison and was on my way back home when I remembered you lived out here. Thought I'd stop by and see what a farmer looks like."

Spence grabbed Clay's hand and pumped it, laughing good-naturedly. "I won't make the cover of *GQ*, but I'm happy and that's worth a lot."

Clay's smile faded at the word *happy*, remembering Fiona's simple wish.

Spence braced his back on the side of Clay's truck. "I hear congratulations are in order."

Clay frowned, ducking his head as he nodded. "Yeah. In fact, that's why I stopped by."

"Needing a little advice on how to handle the wife?" Spence teased.

Clay shook his head. "No. I wanted to make you an offer."

It was Spence's turn to frown. "What kind of offer?"

Clay laid it out for him in the simplest terms possible, explaining about his intention of divorcing Fiona and why he needed to raise the cash.

Spence studied him for a long moment. "I handled quite a few divorce cases during my law career, and I always asked the person who approached me one question before agreeing to handle the divorce."

"What's that?" Clay asked.

"Do you love her?"

The question took Clay by surprise. "Whether or not I love Fiona isn't important," he replied, trying to dodge the question. "It's her happiness that I'm concerned about."

Spence pursed his lips as if considering, then shook his head. "It's a good thing you're asking me to invest in your ranch and not asking me to handle your divorce. If you were, I'd have to say no."

"Why's that?"

"Because where there's love, there's hope, and I never take on a divorce case where there's still hope of a reconciliation."

"There's no hope for Fiona and me," Clay insisted.

Spence snorted and pushed away from the truck. "Then you're as stubborn as you are blind."

"Where are you going?" Clay asked, concerned that Spence had changed his mind about investing in his ranch.

"To get my checkbook," Spence called over his shoulder.

Clay staged his return home to arrive long after Fiona had gone to bed. And he planned to leave before she awoke the next morning. He wanted to avoid any conversation with her until he had all his ducks in a row and was ready to tell her about the divorce.

But he discovered sleeping beside her was impossible. From the moment he slid into bed, he was aware of her. The heat of her body, her scent, the brush of her hip against his when she turned onto her back. But, thankfully, she'd never once awakened.

And Clay had never slept.

Just before sunrise, he slipped from the bed and dressed quickly, determined to leave before she awoke. As he opened the back door, he thought he heard her call to him, but he closed the door quickly and hurried to his truck.

He drove around for more than two hours, waiting until he was certain the Carson household was up for the day, then headed for their ranch. As he parked in front of their mansion and looked up at the grand house, he was reminded what a tremendous step down in lifestyle Fiona had made when she'd married him and moved to his ranch.

More convinced than ever that he was doing the right thing, he climbed down from his truck and approached the front door. He rang the bell, then waited for someone to answer, and was stunned when Ford himself opened the door.

"Clay!" Carson said in surprise, then opened the door wider. "Come in, come in. I'll tell Anita to set an extra plate for breakfast."

"No," Clay said, dragging off his hat and stepping inside. "I just want to talk to you for a moment, if you don't mind."

Already headed for the kitchen, Carson stopped and peered back at him, his brow pleated in a frown. "Is something wrong?"

"No. Not exactly." He gestured with his hat toward Carson's study. "If we could talk in there…"

His frown deepening, Ford turned into his office, waited until Clay entered, then closed the door behind them. He crossed to his desk and sat down behind it. "What's this all about?" he asked.

Clay pulled an envelope from his shirt pocket and tossed it onto the desk. "There's your one hundred thousand."

Carson looked from the envelope to Clay. "But that money's yours. We had an agreement."

Clay nodded. "Yes, sir, we did. But I don't want your money."

"Why not? You earned it. You married Fiona, just as you agreed to do."

"Yes, sir. But I also agreed to teach her responsibility and commitment."

"And have you?"

"I can't take credit for the changes, but she's not the same woman I married. I think you've seen evidence of that."

Carson lifted a brow. "You mean this child-care facility she's all pumped up about?"

"Yes, but this isn't just a whim of hers, if that's what you're thinking. She's committed to the project. And she's displayed tough business savvy while making her plans. She's already gathered enough financial commitments to cover more than half the construction costs, plus she's persuaded an architect to draw up the plans for her for free."

"She's a Carson. I wouldn't expect anything less of her."

Clay nodded, understanding that Carson's gruffness was the man's way of hiding his pride in his daughter's accomplishment.

"Then I'm sure you'll agree that it's time to end the marriage."

Carson's eyebrows shot up. "What? End the marriage. Why?"

Clay settled his hat back on his head and prepared to leave. "Because the mission is accomplished. Fiona has proved that she's responsible, that she understands the meaning of commitment. To continue would be a waste of time for both of us."

Clay could tell by Carson's expression that he didn't agree with his decision, but the man didn't offer any arguments.

He did, however, push the envelope back across the desk. "Keep the money," he muttered. "It's yours. You earned it."

Clay stepped back. "No, sir. I don't want your money. I never felt right about taking it in the first place. But if it'll make you feel better, give it to Fiona. You can tell her it's for her child-care center."

Fiona stared at the long to-do list she held, but couldn't for the life of her concentrate long enough to tackle even the simplest task listed there. She was worried. No. She was beyond worried. She was scared to death.

She'd noticed a change in Clay over the past few days. A definite withdrawal that grew more pronounced with each passing day. At first she'd shrugged off her concerns, blaming his inattentiveness and the long hours he spent away from the house on his work. But she couldn't excuse his behavior any longer. Coming home in the middle of the night and leaving before daybreak without offering her any kind of explanation was inexcusable.

She heard the sound of his truck and lurched to her feet, her gaze going to the clock on the kitchen wall. What was he doing coming home in the middle of the day? she wondered, then hurried to the back door to meet him.

She pushed open the door just as he was climbing the steps. "Hi," she said, hiding her fears behind a welcoming smile. "You're home early."

He stopped, his gaze meeting hers, then he glanced away and pushed past her. "I need to talk to you."

A shiver chased down her spine at the ominous tone in his voice. She dropped her hand from the door, letting it close, and followed him into the den. "What about?"

He stood in the center of the room, facing the dark fireplace, his back to her, his hat in his hand. "I want a divorce."

Her heart dropped, then shot to her throat. "A divorce? But…why?"

"This marriage was only temporary. Surely you must have realized that."

"Yes, but—"

He spun to face her, his face taut with anger. "Don't make this difficult, Fiona. I'm going out of town for a couple of days. I expect you to be gone by the time I get back."

"But, Clay—"

He tossed an envelope onto the chair. "There's the rest of your allowance," he said, then pushed past her and headed for the front door.

She didn't try to stop him. She couldn't. She was too choked with tears to squeeze a word past her throat.

Eleven

Fiona wasted no time packing her things and moving out. She never once considered returning to her parents' home, though she knew they would welcome her with open arms.

She was determined to go forward, not back.

Within hours of Clay leaving, she located a condominium near downtown, put down a deposit using funds from her allowance, then arranged for some of the hands from her father's ranch to help her move her things again. By sundown, there wasn't a sign left at his house to indicate that she'd ever lived there.

She didn't allow herself to cry—at least, not after the buckets of tears she'd shed when he'd first left her. It was easy, she discovered. She simply exchanged all the old feelings she'd had for Clay for hate. He deserved her hatred, she told herself. He'd tricked her into thinking he cared for her, made her fall in love with him. She'd even given him her virginity, considering him worthy of the gift, and he'd tossed her aside like an old pair of boots he'd grown tired of.

Oh, yes, she told herself, it was easy to come up with reasons to hate him. She wiped away the moisture that leaked down her cheeks.

And in time, she was sure she would actually suc-
ceed in feeling the hatred.

Two days later, as he'd stated, Clay returned to Mission Creek. He stopped by the post office downtown,
picked up his mail, then headed for his ranch. As he
turned down a side street, taking a shortcut to the highway, he saw the sign. He pulled to the curb in front
of the vacant lot where it was posted and stared.

She'd done it, he thought, the words on the sign
blurring before his eyes. Fiona had finally come up
with a name for the charitable organization she'd
founded. Sara's Dream. He couldn't imagine a better
way to honor the memory of the little girl whose tragic
death had spawned the idea for the child-care center.

He stared at the sign a moment longer, then dragged
a sleeve across his eyes and pulled back onto the
street. As he did, he remembered that Fiona wouldn't
be there waiting for him this time when he arrived
home. At least, she wouldn't be if she'd followed his
instructions. And he didn't doubt for a minute that she
wouldn't have. He'd been clear in stating his expec-
tations, cruel even.

But the cruelty was necessary, he told himself, as
was his haste in leaving. He'd seen the tears in her
eyes, the hurt he'd caused her. If he'd stayed a second
longer, he'd have gathered her in his arms and told
her he didn't mean it. He would've told her he didn't
want a divorce. That he loved her. That he wanted to
live with her always.

But that would have only bought him time with her, he knew. Eventually she would want out of the marriage. He'd simply saved her the stress of having to ask for the divorce herself and saved her the time she'd have wasted staying married to him.

She'd thank him for it someday, he was sure.

"Well, hi, Daddy," Fiona said in surprise, opening the door of her condominium wider.

Carson strode past her and looked around. He grunted, then swung his gaze to her. "How much are you paying a month for this place?"

Fiona closed the door, then crossed her arms over her chest. "That's none of your business."

"If it's more than a grand, they're stealing you blind."

"I'll be sure to share your opinion with the owner when I pay my next month's rent."

He scowled. "Well? Are you going to invite me to sit down?"

Chuckling, she gestured to a chair. "Have a seat and I'll get us a cup of coffee."

He dropped down on the chair, recognizing it as one he'd once had in his den, before Grace had redecorated the last time. At the thought of his wife, he remembered Grace's fury with him when she'd learned that Clay was divorcing Fiona. He called after Fiona, "Do you have any whiskey you can add to that coffee?"

She returned, carrying a tray with two cups. "Sorry. Only cream or sugar."

He scowled again as he accepted a cup. "Probably holding out on your old man," he muttered, then added under his breath, "Takes after her mother."

Fiona hid a smile as she sat opposite him. "That's odd. Most people say that I take after you."

He dragged a hand over his hair. "Yeah, well. You could do worse."

Fiona relaxed back in her chair. "Did Mother send you over here to check on me?"

He shook his head. "No. In fact, she'll probably skin my ears when she finds out I came without her."

"I take it your visit is of a business nature, rather than a social one."

He placed a hand over his heart, looking wounded. "Do I have to have a reason to drop by and see my daughter?"

She laughed softly. "No. But I assumed, if you came without Mother, you had something on your mind that you didn't want her to know about."

He grimaced. "As a matter of fact, I do." He set aside his coffee cup and reached into his shirt pocket. He tossed a thick envelope onto her lap.

She looked from it to her father. "What's this?"

He waved an impatient hand at her. "Open it and see for yourself."

Frowning, she tore back the flap and looked inside. Her eyes widened in amazement. "Why, there must be thousands of dollars here!"

"A hundred thousand to be exact."

She looked up at her father. "What's it for?"

"Your child-care center."

She pressed her fingers to her lips, touched by his generosity. "Oh, Daddy," she said tearfully, "this is wonderful. Thank you so much."

"Don't thank me. Thank Clay. The money's his."

"Clay?" she repeated in confusion.

He squirmed, knowing he'd just boxed himself into a corner. "Well, yeah. You see…well, I sorta paid Clay to marry you."

"I knew that."

"You did?" he asked in surprise.

"Yes. Clay told me. But why do you have the money and not him?"

He lifted his hands. "The damn fool gave it back. Refused to keep it. Said he'd never felt right about taking it in the first place. Told me to give it to you for the child-care center."

Tears filled her eyes. "Clay said that?"

Her father held up a hand as if taking an oath. "Every word, or my name isn't Ford Carson." His expression growing serious, he leaned over and laid a hand on her knee. "Fiona, what happened? I thought the two of you were getting along just fine."

The tears spilled over onto her cheeks. "I thought we were, too. Then one day he came home and said he wanted a divorce."

"Maybe if I were to talk to him…"

She shook her head. "No. Please, don't. It's over. It was never meant to be anything but a temporary marriage from the beginning. It's best that I accept the fact that he doesn't want me and get on with my life.''

Fiona stepped out of the lobby of the Lone Star Country Club and stopped beneath the portico to turn her cell phone back on. She'd just had lunch with her mother in the Empire Room, and after the second time her cell phone had rung, interrupting their meal and conversation, her mother had insisted that she turn the blasted thing off.

Fiona chuckled, remembering her mother's exasperated look, then sighed and turned her face up to the sun. She was so lucky, she told herself, to have such loving and supportive parents. Though she tried her best to hide her feelings from them, they sensed her pain over the breakup of her marriage to Clay and were doing everything in their power to help her deal with it.

The thought of Clay brought the sting of tears, and she shoved on her sunglasses and headed for the parking lot.

"Fiona!"

She stopped and turned, then smiled when she saw Spence Harrison loping toward her. She waved, waiting for him to reach her, whereupon he wrapped her in a big bear hug. Laughing at his exuberant embrace, she stepped from his arms. "What are you doing in town?"

He gestured toward the clubhouse. "Hoping to see Flynt. Is he here?"

She glanced over her shoulder. "I think so. At least, Mother said she was planning to drop by the office to see him." She turned back to him and smiled. "You look wonderful, Spence. Marriage must agree with you."

He beamed. "I couldn't be happier. I have a wonderful wife, a terrific son. And I'm thoroughly enjoying life on the farm."

Fiona shook her head, amazed by the change in him. "Well, it shows."

His smile slowly faded and he caught her hand, gave it a squeeze. "I was sorry to hear that your and Clay's marriage didn't work out."

She felt the familiar rush of tears and stiffened her shoulders, forcing the emotion back. "Thanks, Spence. That means a lot."

He gave her hand another squeeze, then released it, shaking his head. "I told Clay that it was a damn good thing he asked me to buy into his ranch rather than handle his divorce case, because I sure as hell wouldn't have wanted a part in ending the marriage of two good friends."

She looked at him with puzzlement. "You invested in Clay's ranch?"

He winced. "Sorry," he said guiltily. "I assumed you knew."

She shook her head. "No, but then I haven't spoken with Clay since he told me he wanted a divorce."

He firmed his lips. "The two of you should talk. If you did, maybe you could work out your differences."

Fiona smiled sadly. "There aren't any differences to work out. At least, not on my part."

Spence looked at her curiously. "You were happy with Clay?"

"Very. But obviously he wasn't happy being married to me."

He snorted a laugh. "Could have fooled me."

"What?" she asked in confusion.

He held up his hands. "I've said enough. Talk to Clay," he advised, then gave her another quick hug. "You might discover that there's a lot in your marriage that's worth saving."

Fiona watched Spence walk away, numbed by what he'd said—and what he hadn't said. Was it possible that Clay still cared for her? she asked herself. She stared after Spence, considering the possibility, then shook her head and turned for the parking lot again.

No. Clay didn't love her. Probably never had. He'd only married her to get his hands on the money he needed to save his ranch. She jerked to a stop. But he'd given back the money her father had paid him to marry her. And he'd sacrificed a portion of his ranch when he'd asked Spence to go into partnership with him.

She shook her head and started walking again. That was all fine and good, she told herself. But it still didn't explain why Clay had wanted a divorce.

Clay raked a weary hand through his hair, then donned his hat, before climbing into his truck. What a day, he thought. He'd started the morning off by snapping at the secretary at headquarters and making her cry. If that wasn't bad enough, he'd then given Todd, the Texas Ranger wannabe, a tongue-lashing, when the patrolman had inadvertently contaminated a piece of evidence. By the time Clay had gotten through with him, the poor guy looked like a whipped pup. Neither of the two had deserved Clay's anger. The secretary and Todd had just happened to be in the wrong place at the right time—a time when Clay needed to unload some of his anger and frustration.

His shoulders weighted with guilt, he put the truck in gear and headed for the ranch.

With each mile that brought him closer to home, dread twisted tighter and tighter in his gut. The place that had once been his refuge, his oasis in a cold and uncaring world, no longer held the appeal it once had. He found it more and more difficult to enter the house and, as a result, stayed outside working until darkness drove him inside. By then, he was too exhausted to do anything but shower and crawl into bed.

But sleep was always a long time coming—if it came at all. Fiona haunted his days, his nights. She was everywhere he looked, everywhere he turned. Every time he opened the refrigerator door, she was there before him, looking the way she had that morning he'd come so close to kissing her, wearing that scrap of nothing, her fingers searing his chest. And the den. He never stepped into the room any longer without seeing her sitting on the floor, surrounded by mounds of wrapping paper and ribbon, her face wreathed in smiles.

His bedroom. That was the worst. He could see her sleeping beside him, feel the comforting warmth of her body curled against his, the silkiness of her touch. She'd left her scent on his pillow, in his bathroom, on his clothes. Every breath he took was a reminder, another dagger in his heart.

He pulled up beside the house and stared at it, knowing he couldn't go inside. Not yet. Maybe not ever. She was there inside waiting for him. Her memory. Her ghost. Opening her arms to him, holding him close. Kissing him, touching him. Smiling at him. Laughing with him. Her voice echoed in the empty rooms, taunting him with his loss, his misery.

Swearing, he shoved open the door and climbed out of the truck, slamming the door behind him. Without a backward glance at the house, he strode for the pasture and opened the gate. After shutting it behind him, he shoved his hands into his pockets and began to walk, no destination in mind, just escape. He didn't want to think about her any longer. If he did, he feared he'd go mad.

But her image was there waiting for him at the back fence, poised before a post, a hammer clutched in her fist. She turned, as her name whispered past his lips, and smiled. He could feel the warmth of it on his face, in his heart. He closed his eyes on a groan and spun away. Turning his face to the sky, he dropped to his knees and let out a long, mournful wail.

He'd thought that bamboo cage and the tortures he'd suffered at the hands of his captors was hell, but they didn't come close to matching the pain he felt now.

Loving Fiona and knowing he could never have her was far worse torture. He'd welcome death now, just to escape the pain of losing her, of looking for her but finding nothing but memories.

Fiona sat at the breakfast bar in her condo, staring at the school picture she held. Sara's mother had given Fiona the photograph earlier that afternoon. Fiona intended to have the image of the precious little girl engraved on a brass plaque that would be hung on the front of the child-care center. *Sara's Dream,* she thought proudly, pleased that she could honor the child's life in a way that might save other children from suffering a similar fate.

Setting aside the photo, she rose and wandered aimlessly around the living room, dragging her fingers along the back of the leather chair she had brought with her, then straightening the silk shade of a table lamp. This was her home now, but it didn't feel like home. But neither did her parents' home when she visited them there. Her heart yearned for Clay's small stone ranch house, with its faded linoleum floors and its beige-painted walls. She laughed softly, remembering her horror when Clay had pulled up in front of the house after the drive back from Mexico, and the car's headlights had shone on the exterior. She'd followed him into the house, praying the interior held more promise. It hadn't.

But sometime during the weeks that followed, she'd developed an affection for the house, and its drabness had no longer bothered her. Not that she wouldn't change a thing or two if she had continued to live there, she told herself. And the first thing she'd do would be to paint those hideous walls.

But she didn't live there any longer, she reminded herself, nor would she ever live there again.

Saddened by the thought, she stopped in front of the wall of built-in bookcases and folded her arms across her chest, studying the titles of the books she'd placed there. Her gaze settled on the spine of the leather photo album her parents had given her and Clay. Though she knew looking at the pictures inside would be painful, she reached up and pulled the album from the shelf.

Tucking her feet beneath her, she sat down in the leather chair and opened the album over her lap. The first picture drew tears. She touched a finger to Clay's cheek, remembering every detail of the evening. The way he'd looked striding toward her, his gaze fixed on her as if she was the only person in the room. The shock she'd felt at that first kiss. The melting of her body against the muscled wall of his when he'd pulled her into his arms for the first dance. "Unforgettable." That was the song they'd danced to and it perfectly described the rest of the weekend.

She dashed away the tears beneath her eyes and turned the page, her heart breaking a little more as she remembered her wish at the fountain. Happiness. Such a simple wish. And for a while, she'd thought they were happy.

She stared at the picture, remembering her conversation with Spence and wondering again what he'd meant when he said, "Could have fooled me." Had Clay been happy married to her? If not, he'd certainly fooled her, as well.

Then she remembered Spence's parting comment, urging her to talk to Clay. What would it help? she asked herself miserably, then tensed.

But what possible harm would it do if she *did* talk to him?

She closed the album and set it aside, then rose, her mind whirling. She wouldn't call him, she told herself as she paced. A conversation as important as the one she planned to have with him required nothing less than a face-to-face confrontation. Should she go to the ranch and talk to him there? Frowning, she shook her head. He'd never let her past the front door.

She snapped her fingers, an idea coming to her, and turned for the breakfast bar where she'd left her cell phone. She'd need help to pull it off, she told herself. Lots of help. And she'd start with her brother, Flynt.

Fiona gave the ends of the plush robe's belt a tug, cinching the garment at her waist. With one last look in the mirror to check her appearance, she grabbed the boom box and headed for the lobby of the spa. In the doorway she paused, looked both ways, then darted out into the night.

She wove her way along the path that led to the adult pool, staying close to the shrubbery and the concealing shadows they offered. She didn't want to be seen. At least, not yet.

She arrived at the pool on schedule and used a key to unlock the iron gate. Once inside, she crossed to the edge of the pool, then turned to make sure she had a good view of the security light in the parking lot.

She knew she'd spend the rest of her life returning the favors she'd gotten for this one night. Her brother, Flynt, alone would make her pay dearly for his part in making the call to Clay and asking Clay to meet him at the Men's Grill. Then there were the staff members of the club whom she'd persuaded to help her with her plan. They'd provided keys to the spa and the security gate at the pool, lent her the robe she was wearing and promised not to breathe a word of her scheme.

But the success of her plan hinged on timing. She gave her watch a nervous glance, then craned her neck to peer at the golden glow of the parking lot's security light again. When the light went out, then came back on, it would be her signal that her performance was to begin.

Wiping her hands down her robe to remove the nervous perspiration from her palms, she began to pace. He'd come, she told herself. She just knew he would. There was no reason for him to refuse Flynt's invitation. Clay liked Flynt and Flynt liked Clay. And there was no reason for Clay to suspect that Fiona was behind the invitation. Why would he? She hadn't seen or spoken to him in the six days since he'd told her to move out.

She caught herself wringing her hands and forced them to her sides. Enough, she told herself, and marched to the boom box. If her plan worked, it worked. And if it didn't...

She gave the knob on the boom box an angry twist and loud music blasted from the built-in speakers. She wouldn't think about what would happen if her plan *didn't* work, she told herself, straightening. She'd worry about that tomorrow.

She crossed back to the edge of the pool and turned to watch the light. She concentrated hard on not blinking, fearing she would miss the dimming of the light. When her eyes began to burn, she blinked quickly, then focused them again.

The light went off and she held her breath, waiting for it to flash on again. When it did, she whipped off the robe and dived into the pool.

Twelve

Clay walked slowly along the stone pathway that led to the Men's Grill, his hands shoved deeply into his pockets. He'd been tempted to tell Flynt that he couldn't meet him at the grill and offer some flimsy excuse for his inability to do so. But in the end, he'd agreed, deciding that anything was better than staying at home.

As he passed by the row of shrubbery that separated the pathway from the adult pool, he glanced in the direction of the pool and frowned at the loud, heavy-metal music coming from within the enclosed area.

"Crazy kids," he muttered under his breath, and swung around, heading back for the gate to the pool area. By golly, as soon as he met up with Flynt at the grill, he was going to insist that Flynt have the club install a higher security fence around the pool or increase the number of guards on patrol, before somebody was hurt and the club was slapped with a hefty lawsuit. Teenagers were dumber than cows and rarely thought about safety. More than likely those in the pool now were half-soused and looking for ways to get themselves into trouble. But Clay knew he'd never be able to live with himself if he ignored their blatant disregard for the rules posted in plain sight for everyone to see and one of them drowned.

When he reached the gate, he braced a hand on it, intending to vault over, but nearly fell on his face when the gate swung open beneath his hand. Surprised that one of the staff members had forgotten to lock the gate when they closed the pool for the day, he stepped out onto the flagstone skirt surrounding the pool. He frowned up at the sky, wishing there was a full moon to offer him some visibility.

With a shrug, he turned and followed the sound of the music to a boom box propped on the end of a lounge chair. He switched it off, then cautiously approached the edge of the pool. He heard the soft splash of water, but couldn't make out the shapes in the pool.

Cursing his lack of a flashlight, he squared his shoulders. "Everybody out," he said in a voice he knew from experience had the ability to make hardened criminals sing like birds. "The party's over."

"Clay? Is that you?"

His heart slammed against his chest. He focused on the spot where he'd heard the voice and squinted against the darkness, sure that his ears were playing tricks on him. "Fiona?"

"Yes, it's me."

He could just make out the shape of her head and shoulders above the dark water. "What the hell are you doing in there?"

"Swimming. Want to join me?"

A vision formed in his mind of another time he'd

caught Fiona swimming here. Then she'd been nude. He prayed to God she wasn't now.

"No, I certainly don't. Now get yourself out of there before someone comes along and sees you."

"Uh-uh."

Already turning away, Clay spun back around, stunned that she would defy him. "What did you say?"

"I said, uh-uh."

He set his jaw. "Fiona, get out of that pool, and I mean *now*."

"Uh-uh."

His blood began to boil. "I don't know what you're trying to prove with this crazy stunt, but I want you out of that pool by the time I count to three. Understand? One. Two—"

"Clay?"

"What?" he snapped in frustration.

"If you want me, you're going to have to come in and get me."

He curled his hands into fists at his side. "Damn you, Fiona. I ought to—"

"Clay?"

He dropped his head to his hand on a groan and rubbed at the headache that had throbbed to life between his eyes. "What?"

"Remember the last time you caught me here swimming?"

Able to recall every intimate detail of her nude

body, he shuddered. "Yes," he murmured wearily. "I remember."

"I wasn't wearing a swimsuit."

"Yeah, I know."

"I'm not wearing one now, either."

Her voice had dropped an octave between one confession and the next. It was huskier now, more seductive. The sound of it flowed through him like whiskey, warming his insides and dulling his mind.

"Fiona," he began desperately, sure that she was purposely trying to drive him mad.

"Come on in, Clay. The water's great."

He stared at the shadowed form of her head, unable to make out the features of her face. But he didn't need to see her to remember what she looked like. Her presence in his house the past week was proof enough of that. He had only to think her name and an image of her filled his mind.

Without even knowing why he was doing it, Clay found himself toeing off his boots and peeling off his socks. Straightening, he heard her soft laughter as he stripped off his jacket and drew his shoulder holster and gun over his head to set aside. The sound of her laughter echoed in his mind as he dived into the water, a siren's song in the darkness that drew him to her. He surfaced within feet of her, now able to make out the features of her face.

Her beauty was breathtaking, heartbreaking. He tread water, staring, not daring to draw any closer for fear he would find she was nothing but a mirage, which would vaporize if he found the courage to touch her. He saw that tears gleamed in her eyes, noted the tremble of her lower lip and wondered at them.

"You came."

Her words were a choked whisper and filled with so much emotion, so much longing, he felt them to the core of his being.

"Fiona—" he said, then stopped, unsure what he'd intended to say.

"I love you, Clay," she whispered.

He stiffened. "No," he said, shaking his head. "You don't love me."

"I do!" she cried.

"You don't!"

She reached out, her touch nothing more than the hesitant brush of a fingertip against his cheek, yet he crumpled, as if she'd hit him with a strong right to the jaw.

"No," he moaned, squeezing his eyes shut against the pleasure of her touch, the need to hold her. "Please, don't do this."

He felt a surge of water against his chest and opened his eyes to find she had moved and was now only inches from him.

"Tell me you don't love me," she said, her lip quivering.

He stared into eyes as green as new spring leaves and saw the pain there, the hope, the need. He shook his head, pushing her hand away from his face. "No, Fiona. No."

"Say it!" she demanded. "Say it, and I'll let you go and never bother you again, I swear."

He opened his mouth to voice the lie, but the words wouldn't come. He shook his head. "It doesn't matter how I feel about you, Fiona. You don't need me. You never did."

Her eyes flashed, then turned hard. "How dare you think you know my needs better than I. I love you. Not at first. My love for you grew slowly. And you grew to love me, too. I know you did."

He gathered his strength around him like a shield to safeguard his heart, while trying his best to protect hers. "Fiona, do you have any idea how much you've grown over the last few weeks, how much you've changed? You've only just begun to discover your capabilities, your talents. You can do anything you set your mind to, be anyone you want to be. If you stayed married to me, it wouldn't be long before you realized how much you'd sacrificed, how much you'd lost. Then you'd begin to resent me. Maybe not at first. But at some point in the future you'd regret having married me and want out."

He waited for some kind of response from her. Something, anything to indicate that she understood. But she simply stared, her chest rising and falling in deep, angry breaths.

When she did speak, her words cut through him like a knife.

"I always thought you were brave," she said, her voice accusing. "Courageous, bigger than life. But you're nothing but a coward. I'm amazed they even let you wear the Texas Ranger badge."

"Now wait just a damn minute, I—"

"No," she shot back, "*you* wait. I love you. I know that and I'm willing to admit it. And I know, too, that you love me. But you are so afraid I'm going to leave you, that at some undefined point in time I'm going to break your heart, you won't allow yourself to believe that I could truly love you. Well, I do," she said, her voice rising in both tempo and emotion. "Whether you choose to believe me or not, I love you and always will."

Clay gulped, not wanting to trust her, yet wanting desperately to do nothing less. "Fiona…"

She sniffed. "What?"

"I love you."

She froze, her arms stilling in the water, her eyes growing wide. When she began to sink, she tread water again. "Wh-what did you say?"

"I love you." He smiled, unable to believe how good it felt to say those three words, then said them again, simply because he could. "I love you."

She pushed out a hand. "No! Wait!" She latched on to his arm and started swimming one-armed for the other end of the pool, dragging him behind her.

When she reached shallow water, she stood and released him. "Now say that again."

"What? That I love you?"

She gulped, nodding. "Yes, that."

He looped his arms low on her waist and pulled her

toward him. "Fiona Carson Martin, I love you with all my heart."

She brought her hands to her face, templing them over her nose and mouth, her eyes brimming with tears. "Oh, that is so sweet. So incredibly sweet."

Lights blazed overhead.

Clay winced, throwing up a hand to protect his eyes. "What the hell?"

"Fiona?" a voice called from the shadows.

Fiona huffed in exasperation. "Not now, Flynt!" she shouted. "He's just getting to the good part."

Another light blinked on, this time the fixture embedded in the pool wall at the opposite end.

Clay immediately grabbed Fiona and shoved her farther under the water, trying to hide her nudity.

"Turn out that damn light!" he ordered angrily.

There was a spattering of laughter, then the pool light was snuffed out. Clay turned slowly to frown at Fiona. "How many people knew about this, besides your brother?"

She hunched her shoulders to her ears and wrinkled her nose. "I don't know exactly. Ten or twelve, I guess."

Clay whipped his head around to peer into the dark shadows beyond the lights. "And they've seen and heard everything."

Since he'd phrased his concern as a statement rather than a question, Fiona didn't bother to respond. Which was just as well. He'd probably strangle her if he knew that she'd fudged a bit on the number. She'd enlisted the aid of at least twenty people to assist her with her plan to get Clay to admit that he loved her.

The overhead lights snapped off, plunging them into darkness again.

"We're leaving now, Fiona," Flynt called.

"Thanks, Flynt," she called back.

"Bye, Fiona."

"Bye, Fiona."

"Check you later, Fiona."

"Don't forget to return the robe to the spa, Fiona," a female voice called.

"And the keys! Don't forget the keys."

The farewells and reminders went on for another full minute before quiet finally settled over the pool area again.

When Clay continued to stare at the darkness, Fiona felt a stab of unease. "You aren't mad at me, are you?"

He turned slowly to face her, his expression incredulous. "Who were all those people?"

"Well, Flynt you already know about," she began. "Then there was Ginger. She lent me the robe from the spa. Phil was there. He was the one who signaled me to let me know when you arrived."

"Signaled you?" he repeated.

"Yes." She turned to point at the parking lot security light. "Phil dimmed the light when you drove through the front gate of the club." She turned back to him. "And George lent me his keys."

"Keys to what?"

"The spa and the gate to the pool area. And I think I heard Victor's voice in there somewhere."

"The massage therapist?"

"Yes. He must have come out of curiosity or maybe support. I don't really know—I didn't ask him to do anything. Oh, and the really deep voice," she continued, "that was Hugo. He was the muscle."

"Muscle?" Clay repeated.

"Yes," she said, looking at him as if surprised that he'd ask the question. "I was nude, after all. If you hadn't shown up, no telling what might've happened to me. Hugo was here if I needed saving."

Clay threw back his head and laughed.

She peered at him curiously. "What's so funny?"

He hugged her to him. "You are. I've never known a woman who had the ability to move a mountain without lifting so much as a finger."

She dropped her mouth open. "I did so lift a finger! I planned the whole thing, plus, may I remind you, I was the one who stripped down to nothing and treaded water for I don't know how long just to make you notice me."

"Oh, I noticed you all right," he said, bringing her hips to his. "But you don't have to strip for me to do that."

A smile of wonder spread across her face. "Really?"

"Yes, really."

She threw her arms around him and squeezed him tight. "Oh, Clay. I'm so happy right now I could cry."

He pushed back to look at her. "Will you be happy living out on the ranch with me?"

She caught his face between her hands and looked deeply into his eyes, showing him her heart. "I wouldn't want to live anywhere else."

He covered her hands with his. "Then let's go home, Fiona. Let's go home."

* * * * *

One

"Oh, hell, you *can't* be serious."

Tyler Murdoch muttered the words aloud even though there was no one to hear.

He squinted against the sunlight—particularly bright and unrelenting as it reflected against the limitless expanse of arid land surrounding the minuscule airfield—and focused on the woman who'd just stepped outside. There was only one small patch of shade afforded by the utilitarian building that served the *aeropuerto* and she'd paused in it. But that didn't mean he couldn't see her just fine.

He pretty much wished he couldn't see her just fine. Then he could pretend she wasn't the person he was there to meet.

Despite the checklist in his hand, he looked her way again. No way could she be the linguistics expert he was to hook up with before flying down to Mezcaya. No…damn…way.

But he had a bad feeling in his gut that she was.

And Tyler Murdoch trusted his gut instincts. They'd kept him alive too many times in his thirty-five years of life to be disregarded now just because he didn't like the way that woman looked standing over there in that patch of shade. Besides, he'd checked the airfield from east to west and knew that the site was secure. The dust-coated SUV that had arrived and hastily departed only minutes ago had been exactly the vehicle that Tyler had been watching for. There was no reason for anyone else to be here at this carefully and deliberately abandoned airfield other than the person he was there to meet.

He managed not to swear a blue streak and looked away from her to focus on the clipboard in his hand. But he knew the checklist of supplies by heart and all he saw in his mind was the woman.

No, he didn't like the way the woman looked. The last thing he needed was to be distracted by some female on an op this important. Westin's life depended on Tyler. There was no damn way he'd fail his former commander; he owed the man too much.

None of which alleviated the impatience rising in him or his annoyance with his superiors for sticking him with that woman. Everyone knew he didn't like working with females. He didn't care what that said about him. He wasn't interested in being politically correct, nor was he particularly concerned with equality between the sexes. As far as Tyler was concerned, a woman could sell out her country just as easily as a man.

God knows Sonya had.

He reached through the open door of the plane and tossed the clipboard into the cockpit where it landed next to the captain's seat. His seat.

He might be in charge of this expedition down to Mezcaya, but he was well and truly stuck with Miss Universe over there in the shade.

He'd been told his linguistics expert was a native of Mezcaya who'd been in embassy service for a while, but Tyler was damned if he could see how. From this distance, she looked too young to have done much of anything. Except maybe graduate from college. Maybe.

But then, Sonya hadn't exactly been decrepit with age, either, and she'd managed to cause plenty of damage.

Disgusted with thoughts that were too old to be plaguing him now, Tyler spun on his heel and strode toward the building. He had a mission to accomplish, and no one, particularly a beautiful woman, was going to get in his way.

SILHOUETTE Romance™

Escape to a place where a kiss is still a kiss...
Feel the breathless connection...
Fall in love as though it were
the very first time...
Experience the power of love!

Come to where favorite authors—such as
Diana Palmer, Stella Bagwell,
Marie Ferrarella and many more—
deliver heart-warming romance and genuine
emotion, time after time after time....

Silhouette Romance—
stories straight from the heart!

Silhouette®
Where love comes alive™